THE
SIX-G

G·K Hall &Co.

Also by Nelson Nye in Large Print:

Born to Trouble
Gunman, Gunman
The Lonely Grass
Mule Man
Not Grass Alone
The Parson of Gunbarrel Basin
Quick-Trigger Country
Renegade Cowboy
Riders by Night
Trail of Lost Skulls
Trigger Talk
Trouble at Quinn's Crossing
Wide Loop
Wild Horse Shorty
Wolftrap

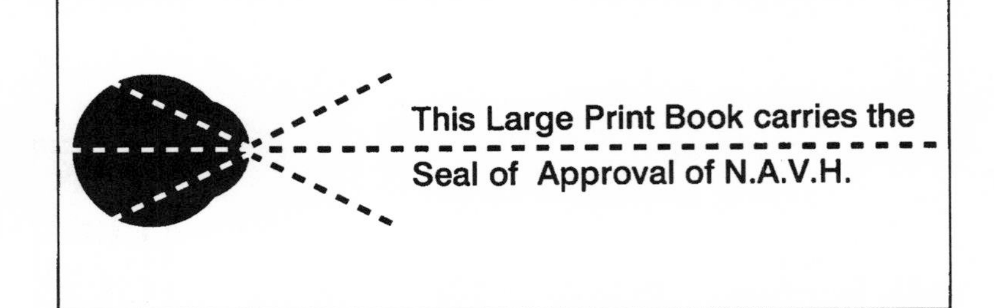

THE SEVEN SIX-GUNNERS

Nelson Nye

G.K. Hall & Co. • Thorndike, Maine

Published in 2000 by arrangement with Golden West Literary Agency.

G.K. Hall Large Print Paperback Series.

The text of this Large Print edition is unabridged.
Other aspects of the book may vary from the original edition.

Set in 16 pt. Plantin by Anne Bradeen.

Printed in the United States on permanent paper.

Library of Congress Cataloging-in-Publication Data

Nye, Nelson C. (Nelson Coral), 1907–
The seven six-gunners / Nelson Nye.
p. cm.
ISBN 0-7838-9179-2 (lg. print : sc : alk. paper)
1. Tombstone (Ariz.) — Fiction. 2. Treasure-trove — Fiction.
3. Large type books. I. Title.
PS3527.Y33 S4 2000
813′.54—dc21 00-057576

THE SEVEN SIX-GUNNERS

I

It didn't seem like any handful of months could have made so much difference in the way a place shaped up. The huddled blobs of buildings appeared almost to have settled against each other like an armlock of staggering men in their cups. They sure as sin looked punier than they had to me last winter when I'd come through here chasing cow thieves. Even in the dark they had a scurvy of dilapidation that came at you like a smell.

Made me think first off I'd got turned around. I hadn't. This was Allen Street. There was the Crystal Palace and Hatch's, the Alhambra and the Occidental and, across the way, the Grand and Cosmopolitan hotels and Warner Brothers' huge barn of a store. Tombstone, all right. I sat back in my saddle trying to make out what had happened.

One big difference was the astonishing quiet.

Tombstone had never been modest about noise. The bang and reverberating boom of its stamps pounding raw ore into powder had served merely to puncturate its other rackets. This had been a bull roarer of a town, never shut down and crammed with carousals, horseplay and bickering. Where were the Cousin Jacks and the cowboys, the shouts and drunken laughter, the crash of jerked pistols and the damned fiddle squeal — the five-abreast riders that had torn through these streets?

It was hard to believe I was in the same place.

Lemon halos of lamplight gleamed uncertainly behind the grimed windows of maybe a dozen establishments. A paltry nothing beside the glare when forty thousand leaps of flame had turned the night skies red as paint and guns had blazed around the clock as hordes of shouting sweaty fools had schemed and cursed and toiled and brawled over the gangrenous metals ripped from this earth.

Tradition of that kind rooted deep and not likely to be snuffed in eight short months. Not even the Earps had very much changed it, rough as they'd been in the wink of their shooters. Nor Curly Bill Brocious and all his hellions — or even Burt Mossman, fierce as he'd been.

So what could have turned this town so still? It was like a plague had swept the place.

I came out of the saddle, standing stiffly down, the slanch of my glance darkly quartering the street. A window flapped someplace in a lift of the wind but no talk prowled the raddled gloom.

Ducking under the pole, I stepped up on

planks that were frazzled by rowels and the track of sped bullets. As far down Allen as a feller could see the street was an abandoned aisle of stacked shadows. Gave a man a queer turn, no getting around it.

The place had been called too tough to die. Yet just over there, against the slant of racks, two horses stood hipshot asleep on their feet where only last winter half a hundred had been.

Had me fighting my hat, I can tell you.

A dim sheen of light leached through unscrubbed windows at either side of the Oriental's doorhole. Outside this deadfall, about where I was standing, Luke Short had killed Charlies Storms one night. Scarcely ten steps beyond, behind that corner, Buckskin Frank Leslie had shot Billy Claibourne. The town was pocked with such reminders. Boot Hill, up yonder, was crammed with old bones and if there was one thing I wasn't hankering for it was to have mine added to that moldering pile.

I'm Flick Farsom, happens you've been wondering. Late of the Lincoln County War that busted up Murphy-Dolan, killed Alex McSween and just about finished Old Man Chisum who had figured to be about the biggest damn thief ever to come out of Texas.

I could of stayed over there I guess if I'd wanted. The Kid was dead and Lew Wallace had give out a blanket pardon to get things patched up as best he could. But old animosities have a way of hanging on and I had just about got my belly full. A gent doesn't cotton to putting in his whole time with his back to a wall.

Like enough I'm what you would call a rolling stone. Fiddlefooted, some have said, and they're probably right — or were when they'd said it. Man gets tired of that after a while. What I'd really been hunting these past several months was a good quiet place where I could drop out of sight. When a gent knows little beyond cattle and guns, finding a hole he can cram himself into just ain't so danged easy as might be imagined.

I'd gone to Texas, plumb into the brasada — which is country where brush gets so thick and stout you pack an axe just to get yourself through. Happened some others seemed to have got the same notion, some of that Jingle-bob crowd that had rode for John Chisum. Would of been a short life if I had hung around there. I moseyed clean north to Kansas.

I tried breaking horses. But when a ranny gets hip deep into his twenties he can't take that kind of thing like he used to. I drove stage for a spell, halfway figuring to stick till a couple damned fools in the rain one night stepped out of the dark with lifted rifles. Toting them fellers in had soured me some.

Colorado that had been. Now I was down to the bottom of Arizona, said to be the wildest west of Forth Smith. It didn't look wild to the clabber-headed chump who had told Major Murphy he'd just as lief shoot Billy the Kid.

I wasn't figuring to step into another jackpot like that.

The Oriental's louvered doors, agleam within that shadowed entrance, spilled yellow light across the walk's gray planks. No piano trinkled out, no clink of glass or conversations. Only thing I could see, looking in, was the bent-over shine of some jasper's bald head.

Few lessons had been ground deeper into me than caution but nobody, far as I knew, would expect me here. It was all very well and even smart to be careful but this kind of thing, given into continuous, could turn a man into a goddam rabbit.

Squaring my shoulders, I pushed open the doors.

The place was only a little less embalmed than I'd figured. No need to line up to get your boot on the rail. This bald-headed joker — evidently the apron — appeared to be anchored to the sober side of the bar. The games were closed, dust enough on the green cloths to make them seem gray. Only other person I could see, besides this jigger holding down the mahogany, was a black-haired female with the top of her bent over a beer at a table.

Neither of them bothered to see who'd come in.

The remembered pictures still looked down from the walls, cheap and tawdry in the lamp's feeble light. All the corners was filled with shadows. Even the mirrors looked foggy and dull.

The barkeep finally got up off one elbow. "What's yours, Mac?"

"Being's you've asked me, bourbon," I said. "What's come over this town?"

He set out a bottle, put a glass beside it from a mound of the same behind him. "Old age, I reckon." He wagged his forehead against braced knuckles and paraded his teeth in a prodigious yawn. "Catches up with the best of us."

"Where's the Earps?"

"Gone. Cleared out. Lock, stock an' barrel."

"You don't mean to tell me." I picked up the bottle, took a considering squint and thought what a sight that must have been. On a par with the Hebrew children quitting Egypt. "Whole town go with 'em?"

"There's a few hangin' on. Don't ask me why."

"Place," I said, "looked pretty lively last winter."

He gave me a closer scrutiny. "You musta been through early. Before the water got into 'em." He shoved a hand toward the bottle. "You goin' to drink that stuff or . . ."

The hand hung fire while we eyed each other. "You mean," I said, "all the mines have closed down?"

"All the ore worth workin' is plumb under water. An' like to stay there if you want my opinion."

"Oh, it's not that bad," a crippled codger piped up, limping in from the back with a broom and bucket. "Plenty of folks still around. Not a sportin' crowd, I'll give in to that, but once they git things opened up again —"

"That'll be the day!" The bald barkeep snorted.

The old coot set up his broom like a hitching post. "Now, Ollie, you got to admit they're workin' on it. That engineer from the T. M. & M. said —"

"His job holds out just as long as the hopes, an' you can bet your bottom dollars he ain't about to cut himself off at the pockets."

"Len Mosslin claims the Old Guard mine and the Bunker Hill will both be goin' by the end of the month."

"He say which month?"

The old man, shaking his head, limped off and the bald-headed Ollie, dragging a rag across his bar, said like Moses handing down the twelve stones, "Them mines is plumb finished."

"What about pumps?"

He threw up his hands.

"Well," I said, picking up my glass, "maybe they'll open some new ones."

It was no skin off my butt. Some fellers just naturally rub a gent wrong, and this contentious old codger with his windy pronouncements had about took my mind clean away from good sense. The woman piped up then. "Work . . . is it work you're looking for?" she asked.

I tossed off my drink. "Just passing through."

But I could feel her eyes.

I picked her up in the mirror. Pretty pert proposition. Hair as black as the ace of spades. Black eyes, too. Mexican or Basque — might even be Spanish. I'd seen her kind before in dives but something about her was somehow different, and it wasn't the pride because a lot of them have that.

Or make out to have.

There was paint on her mouth but her clothes had some class and her skirts was too long to have been much around a bar. In the glass our eyes swapped a couple of looks and it was like she had put a hand on my shoulder. Then her glance pulled away.

She finished her beer. She got the shawl off the back of her chair and stood up. And she knew how to stand to let you know what she had was every bit of it real and oiled for action. She fixed the shawl over her hair, took up her reticule and left.

"Dames!" the barkeep said, rolling his eyes.

"Reckon a man could find him a room in this town?"

"You kiddin'?"

I dropped some silver on the bar. "Old Dick Clark still around?"

"Them fancy Dans was the first to go. Then the pimps an' their whores an' the hard-rock crowd." He hoisted one side of his lip like a horse. "What'll you give fer this place, — cash on the barrelhead? C'mon, name a price."

"I'm just huntin' quiet — not a coffin," I said.

Outside in the dark, crossing the planks toward my dun, I marveled again at the way this wild town had so suddenly tamed. Anyone predicting such a change last winter would have been laughed at for loco.

It kind of made a man think.

I was still wrassling it around when I went under the rail. Coming up, straightening, reaching for the reins, a voice someplace in the shadows said, softly, "Just a minute."

It was her.

She stepped out from behind my horse but not so far as to come into the light. A smell of crushed violets lifted off the dark shape of her. "Would you take a job, Mr. Farsom . . . if you got out of it what you wanted?"

I looked at her, hard.

"How'd you know my name?"

I couldn't tell what she was doing in the dark — for all I knew she might be pointing a gun at me. She didn't answer straight off. Then she said, holding her voice down, "I have an uncle at Lincoln. I was there when the Kid got out of that window."

I said, "I still don't see —"

"They were expecting you to shoot him."

"But . . ." I said, kind of riled and impatient, "How'd you know *just now?*"

"I remembered your voice."

Some guys, I expect, would have been some set up — a looker like her. Alls I could feel was that mess I'd got into. There might be those holed up in these parts that would damn well like to see me planted.

I said, "What kind of a job?"

She come a step forward, likely figuring her nearness would work some advantage. Or maybe she come for a closer communion, having no thought of the hungers she stirred. It was too dark to see, where she stood, what her look was.

The stillness got thick with the chirking of crickets.

"What sort of job?"

"Well . . . nothing," she said with her breath so close herded I had to crane over, "nothing that would bother a man like you."

"Gun work," I growled on an outrushing breath.

She knew me all right. She held quiet for a bit, maybe turning it over. "I don't imagine it will come to that? All I want is . . . protection. You will help me, won't you?"

I eyed the dark shape of her, the distrust still on top.

The throaty sound of her reached out, curling round me stronger than wine. She said, "Write your own ticket," and the words rang a bell, chousing up thoughts a man my age shouldn't of took no stock in. That crushed violets smell of her was like warm hands sliding through my guts.

I pulled back, thinking I had better hit leather, better dig for the tules the way I'd been minded. But like a damn nump I kept right on standing there.

What come off my tongue was the kind of fool talk you'd expect from a kid. "What are you scairt of?"

"That's just it — I don't know."

I kept staring.

She dragged in a deep breath. I watched the way it pushed out the front of her.

"It's just a feeling." She sighed. "Cold fingers running up and down my back."

I had some fingers that would like to do that. "Where is this job? What's it pay, and —"

"About forty miles. In the Davis Mountains."

"Never heard of 'em."

Sounding bitter, she said, "The lonesomest hole I ever got into. Nothing but rocks and snakes and cactus. A place God forgot and never bothered to finish."

"When do we start?" I said, feeling better.

II

I must have been born with the simples. I should have got clean away, just as quick and as far as a fast horse could take me. My steeple never had been crowded with bells but even a chap in three-cornered pants might of savvied this dame wasn't up to no good with her perfumery and paint and all that clack she had give me. Why, those damn Davis mountains wasn't even on a map. But alls I could think of was the isolation of it — a place that had nothing but rocks, snakes and cactus. It figured to be just the hole I was hunting.

There was, of course, one other thing that had considerable to do with my foolishness — her. I reckon I don't know a great deal about women, but it wasn't just her looks. There was other things too . . . the queer kind of breathless way she spoke, the husky sound of her voice — even the way she stood, and the half glimpsed things that peered from her eyes.

Lavender gloves came almost at her elbows. Lithe and slim she was in a quail-colored dress that fit tight at her neck. Her waist I could of got my two hands around — and did when I helped her into the rig, a kind of two-wheeled cart or cut-down buckboard the like of which I had never seen before.

We got started straightaway. She was hoping, she said, to get home in time for breakfast. Climbing onto the dun I followed her out, content to ride behind for a spell but planning, even then, to be up on that seat with her before we got done.

This I mention to show you the state I was in, lally-gaggin along with my head full of wool and never a thought for what direction we was headed. I did get to wondering what her father might be like. Certainly he figured to be a pretty big man.

It was right about there, with all that craziness in me, that the first disquiet began to nib at my attention. For all I knew he could be poor as Job's turkey.

The night wasn't so dark now we'd lost the lights. About ten million stars was winking down. Even without no moon a feller could make out well enough where he was going. She handled that team like she'd been brought up to it.

Nothing strange about that. Most women raised on a ranch could handle horses. Yet it did seem queer, her being off like this so far from home all by herself. This was a gringa fashion and she didn't look gringa, not even in this starshine.

Odd, too, where I'd found her. Guzzling beer in a saloon.

Plenty of Mexican girls did that, but not the kind that come from big holdings. No hidalgo or don would put up for a minute with having his women folks carrying on so common.

Sure, she might have run off. Some of those girls was wild as March hares.

I got to working back through the things she had said, surprised to find so little to catch hold of. Big thing I come up with was her being so frightened — yet she hadn't said that, not in so many words, She hadn't actually said 'ranch' when you come right down to it. Hadn't told me her name. Alls she had said was I should call her Lupita. I thought back to the look that had come along with it.

The rattle and clank and the clopping of hoofs didn't rush up so loud now we'd got off the shale. We was down in a kind of broad trough, a sort of canyon, with the thorned wands of wolf's candle showing on the slopes among a scattering of pear and greasewood. The lean bright sickle of a moon glowed like silver about one foot above the wall's ragged rim.

We'd been riding some longer than I'd figured by this sign, and the chill of the night was beginning to leach into me. "What's the name of this place we're headed for?"

I watched the turn of her head as she came half around. She didn't answer right off but kept looking like maybe she was rolling something over in her mind. Whatever she saw, I got the notion she liked it. Her teeth flashed.

"Silver Spring," she said.

"A ranch?"

Again she seemed to take longer than was needed. "I suppose," she said, "you could call it that. We don't have any cattle."

"Not a *sheep* spread, is it?"

I heard her silvery tinkle. "We're running horses."

What there was about that to make her laugh I couldn't see. But it was plain enough, even to me by now, she wasn't the kind to talk a guy's arm off. Way she measured out information you'd have thought it was gold sliding out of her fingers. "Mustangs?" I said.

I caught the glint of her teeth as she touched up the team. Good horses, that pair. Matched bays. Looked like Morgans.

The moon got up. I found the north star. Begun to seem like we was headed southwest, though it was hard to pin down what with twists and all the dodging and turning we done to keep from ramming into rocks. Way this girl handled the ribbons was a caution. She seemed to know where she was every bump of the way. Myself, I couldn't even begin to see a trail, neither wheel marks nor horse tracks. When I mentioned this she said it was the winds. "Loose sand through here. Always shifting and changing."

"This the only way in?"

"You don't have to worry. We're not going to be lost."

Well, lost was what I'd come out here for and it

begun to look like I'd come to the right place. I said, "This ain't the Jornada, is it?"

"Not really." She spoke up quick enough answering that, but she hadn't just give it to me right off the cuff. She appeared to measure every word, to look askance at every question. The queerness of it begun to dig through the spell of her nervousness.

As the night unraveled the terrain got rougher. The whole stretch of this country seemed to lay on some slant like in time before man it had someway faulted, like it had started to flop over and had give out midway.

I hadn't spotted one light in all this riding. Hadn't seen any cows. Usually a man would turn up a few, even in hard-scrabble landscape like this was. Couldn't everyone be cattle barons. Small independents, the one-man layouts and greasy-sackers, generally figured to latch onto whatever was too sorry for the big spreads to bother with — barrens like this where a man pretty near had to go to hell for water. But if there was anyone ranching this end of the cactus they was sure some shy about letting it be known.

Nights in the desert, where you've got any kind of altitude at all, even in the hot months can get surprisingly cold. This one was, with a chill wind pouring down off the rimrocks. Even through my brush jacket I could feel the teeth of it nipping at the ends of me. I asked Lupita if she wanted my fish.

Shaking her head she got into a kind of short waist-length coat that looked like a Confederate shell jacket that she pulled out from under the seat. "I'm not really minding it," she said, tugging a lap robe over her knees.

I debated getting into the slicker myself, figuring it would turn at least the worst of this wind that was beginning to blow now in grit-laden gusts. I pulled the wipe over my nose, deciding to tough it out for the sake of having a more easy access to my guns, the one under my leg and the pistol riding my hip. By which you will see I was not entirely easy in my mind, though I hadn't yet got around to taking conscious stock of it.

"How did you happen," she asked presently, "to be around Tombstone?"

That was a pretty open question and not one generally asked in my circles. "Just sifting around." I shrugged. A woman, of course, was like to ask anything. "You know how it is with us rannies. Just natural born drifters. What's beyond the next hill always seems more fetching than the dirt you got under your toenails."

We rocked along for a spell without no more talk while the unrest that was in me began to build up some. I've been, I suppose, what you might call a trained observer. This could likely be said for any of the bunch that come out of that Lincoln County fracas. Rolling rocks over some poor fool, digging out graves for gents that got careless, had taught plenty of galoots the value of keeping their eyes skun. Still, I wasn't actually suspicious. It was habit, I guess, that was sawing my nerve ends, and becoming a disquiet that was gradually beginning to scratch at my notice.

I didn't climb onto that seat like I'd aimed to. I put in my time looking over the country and it was something to look at, all standing on end. Rock and sand and saguaros and cholla — about as desolate a region as I'd ever got into. How she found a way through with that wagon was something to marvel at, for it didn't look like you could hardly get a horse through.

Along towards morning, with the stars turning pale and a fresh wind stirring, I come out of my silence to rub at cramped muscles. "You got much of a outfit at Silver Spring?"

"We'll be there pretty quick. You can see for yourself."

I done some hard looking, done a mighty mort of it, but alls I could see was the damned rocks and cactus. They was all over everything like flies round a sorghum spill. Then we dropped down into a sort of walled valley and there was this outfit smack dab in front of me.

III

It was about as well hid as the needle somebody lost in a haystack. Even closeup like this you had to stare twice before you realized what you was looking at was buildings, so clever had they been blended with the rock faces tumbled behind them. Holed up here a feller wouldn't need no dog to let him know when company was coming. A gopher couldn't hardly scratch up there without the sound of it raveling through this gulch. For a timid gent it was the finest kind of setup, the one spot of color being the green of the cottonwoods hung out over the house.

Against the door stood a man with a rifle which he didn't put up until Lupita waved. He didn't come off the porch even then. He stayed where he was in blue shadows until she'd drove up and stopped by the steps.

"Morning, Fred. Weren't getting worried, were you?"

She loosed a flutter of laugh and got down, peeling off her gloves while she stomped some of the kinks from her legs. "I've brought back some help. Meet Flick Farsom," she said, waving me up. "A good man with a gun. Flick, shake hands with Fred Oakes. Fred's the boss here at Silver."

He looked me over. I done the same by him. He was probably well into the shank of his forties, dark and bony with a crooked nose whitely ridged with scar tissue. He was built like a stilt. There was a harshness narrowing the displeased search of his stare.

"Grub on the table?" Lupita asked, like it went clean over her head that he was riled. "I could gobble a catamount, hair, claws and all."

Oakes didn't reach out to grab my paw, just stood there meanly sizing me up like a steer he was minded to put on the block. Lupita grinned. "Guess you two will be wanting to talk." She went up the steps and into the house, pulling the plank door shut behind her.

"You the Farsom," Oakes said, "that was mixed up with Murphy?"

"I worked for an L. G. Murphy at Lincoln."

Oakes chewed at this for a couple of minutes, not showing what he thought, not saying nothing either. If he was waiting for me to back off or put up some line about getting the girl home at this time of morning he didn't know as much about me as he let on.

He was gaunt enough to get through a knothole. He had a brushy stubble of gray bristle on his cheeks and the knobs of his hands thumbed onto his shell belt. He said with a bullypuss stare,

"You any kin to Curly Bill Brocius?"

I shook my head.

"Ever met him?"

"Not to know it. Heard he was dead — didn't Earp kill him?"

He give me a dark look, his unwinking stare as hard as a gun snout. "Did he?" Rasping a rope-scarred fist across his whiskers he wheeled, still scowling, and moved towards the door.

"This Brocius," I said, "a particular friend of yours?"

Oakes stopped like he'd heard the cock of a pistol. He didn't come round, didn't get up much wind, but the language he used wasn't no kind for ladies. He chopped it off sudden. "Wash bucket's around to the side."

I can take a hint if it's put to me right. I went around to the side.

When I come back, freshly scrubbed and with my hair slicked down, he was waiting in the door. "We'll tie on the nosebags." Stepping back for me to pass he followed me in.

It was a rangy sort of room, long and lean like Oakes himself, filled with the shadows that come down from the walls. It had a cubbyhole kitchen off to one end and doors leading out to the other parts of the house. A checkered cloth was on a big table in the livingroom proper; benches anchored to either side of it would have seated a crew of twelve. "Set down," Oakes said, "an' bite a biscuit."

The girl had shed her coat. She was at the stove with her sleeves rolled up, filling the place with bacon and coffee smells. I chucked my hat in a corner and got onto a bench while she fetched a heaped platter and come back with the java. While I was turning over my eating tools Oakes settled into a chair at the end.

"Dry summer," he said, fixing a napkin into the neck of his shirt. "How's it been where you come from?"

"I ain't needed webbed feet."

The girl poured our mugs, turned back and fetched the biscuits. She passed Oakes the platter. He took four of the eggs and about half the bacon. There was two eggs left. I took one of them and three crisps of meat. We all got biscuits. They was stacked three deep and flat and hard as crackers.

"This the whole of your outfit?" I said to Oakes.

"I ain't got much help an' that's a fact. Hard to git hands to stick in this country. No neighbors," he said with a dry little grin that someway, I figured, was aimed at Lupita. "Pretty quiet."

The girl tried to stir up some conversation. Oakes' grunts wasn't aimed to encourage it much and I had notions of my own to sort out. When it seemed like I wasn't getting anywhere I started packing my pipe, the old blackened brier I'd carried since Lincoln. The girl's glance touched my face. "More coffee?"

"All right."

Oakes, when she got up to fetch it, was folding

his napkin. He held out his mug. "I'll take some of that."

I put a match to my Durham. "What's the name of your iron?"

"Don't rightly have a name."

"It's a picture brand," Lupita said from the stove. "Cover anything. I knew a man once used to call it the 'Cyclops'."

Oakes got up with his eyes like baked marbles. He didn't look at the girl. Never looked at me either. Just scraped back his chair and stomped off through the door.

I found the girl's eyes. "He'll get over it," she said, and poured me some java. "He's like a bull to get along with till he's had his second snort."

She set the pot back, considered me a moment and then sat down in Oakes' chair. "There's probably some things about this deal you won't like but if you play your cards right . . ."

"I'm weaned," I said. "You can speak right out."

She smiled. "Fred's sour and suspicious and kind of set in his ways. He's had a lot to contend with —"

"He don't want me here."

"Give him a little time," she said.

I scratched a match and puffed for a spell. For some reason she liked the idea of my being around. I was some considerable of that notion myself but it hadn't grown into no mote in my eye. If Oakes was against it it wasn't likely I'd stay. Girl or no girl. And if he was engaged in moving other gents' horses he was flirting with something I didn't want any part of.

"Fred isn't grabbing them," she said, "he just grazes them."

"You can kick as high for a sheep as a goat."

Red lips pulled away from her teeth. "And you were the one that would just as lief shoot Billy."

"I got over that craziness."

"Sure of that, Flick?"

I scowled at the swirls of smoke floating around me.

"You didn't claim amnesty from Governor Wallace. Your name wasn't posted in the lists of those pardoned."

"Never done anything to be pardoned for."

She just sat with that pussycat grin.

I puffed some more. "You calling me a owlhoot?"

Her eyewinkers flapped. She peered at me brightly. "Guess you'll admit there are those that would."

I come onto my feet, shoved away from the table. "Thanks for the grub. . . ."

"Do you *have* to be a fool?"

"I ain't goin' to be no monkey on a stick!"

"All right. Go on. Clear out," she said, like I didn't have sense enough to blow my own nose. "When Chisum's hands, or some of McSween's bunch, catch up with you out in the dark some night just remember what you had here."

I scooped up my hat and reached for the door.

Like a nump I looked back. "What was that?" I said.

"A place where the devil himself couldn't find you."

She had me cold.

So far as I knew there was nobody after me, but a lot of ill will was still blowing around and she'd put her finger right on it. Bounty hunters was prowling the hills, the rimrocks was filled with masterless men. Some of the soreheads out of that Lincoln County War would be a heap overjoyed to line their sights on a man who'd helped spoil a good thing for them. It was a time to tread lightly and there was plenty of us doing it.

When I got outside Fred Oakes was stowing a fresh chaw in his jaw.

His eyes come around like the wheel of a hawk but his voice when he spoke sounded friendly enough. "I've got some stock you might break if you can stand a little dust." He even dredged up a grin before he spat. "You want to look at 'em?"

I couldn't see where it would hurt much to look.

"All right," I said, with the most of my thinking still back in the house. She'd said I could get out of this about what I wanted and, while I figured that was probably spreading it thick, it did seem like the attractions ought to more than offset any edges of unpleasantness growing out of Oakes' dabbling in other folks' horses. I didn't even know he was doing it. About all I could see for sure was that she seemed pretty anxious to have me around.

A man couldn't be expected to get on his ear about a thing like that.

"Fetch your horse," Oakes said. "We'll cut out a couple fresh ones."

Chances was I had him all wrong. He'd had a good thing here, all alone away out in the cactus with a woman as good looking as Lupita.

Following him back through the rocks it did come over me to kind of wonder what was between them. Probably she'd hired him to run this place. Nobody would ever take Oakes for no Mex.

Just as it looked like we'd about reached the back end of this gorge or gulch or whatever it was, we come into a sort of clearing where there wasn't any rocks for pretty near a hundred feet. This was where they had the corrals, three rails high, laced with ocotillo and bound at the uprights with rawhide cured with the hair on. There was two of these pens, roughly oval, the biggest being about forty foot across and, at the moment, empty. The other one had three horses in it. There was a bunkhouse built into the face of the cliff behind.

"Ropers," Oakes said, indicating the horses. "That grulla there is mine. You can throw your hull on either of the others."

It was pretty good looking stock, nothing fancy but as good as you'd find on a working cow spread. I would say they'd average forty dollars apiece, by itself perhaps a bit more for Oakes' grulla which had a long underline and considerable muscle. I said, "It looks like that mouse might git up and go."

Oakes got a bridle and went in and fetched him out. The horse was docile as a kitten. While he was saddling I got the gear off my dun, all but the bridle which I left on to hold him. I took a cotton-rope halter and went after the buckskin which, in this part of the country, is generally called a bayo coyote. He wouldn't let me even get near him.

I come back and got my grass rope. The horse didn't want no part of it. He ducked and turned and weaved and twisted, always keeping some part of the other one between us. There wasn't no chance to get a shot at his head. "All right, son," I said, "you asked for it," and made a underhand cast he stepped right into. He stopped quick enough then. I brought him out on the halter, cinched up, turned my dun in and put up the bars.

"Where you grazing this bunch?" I said.

Oakes grunted. He sure wasn't one for wasting words. We climbed into leather and he led off past the bunkhouse. I didn't see nothing but rocks back there. It looked like the end of the line to me, but each time I figured we'd reached it another twenty feet or so would open up off at a tangent, shut in by rock walls that pretty near pinched together over us but kept leading on, deepening and dropping till I lost all sense of direction.

"This place got a name?" I said.

Oakes didn't even bother to grunt. He never turned his head, but presently, when the walls widened out enough for me to come alongside, he said in a kind of offhand way, "What we're on is an old smuggler trail. Them bones you been seein' come from Mex'kins an' burros. Been a passle of 'em killed here."

"Indians?"

His lips got to moving but all you could hear was the swush-swush of hoofs plowing through deep sand.

I seen right then he was some kind of nut. Not far enough yet off his rocker maybe to be playing with a string of spools, but no sort either any gent would pick to be ramming around in country like this with a six-shooter strapped in easy grab of his fist.

A loony — and her penned up with him away off here! Small wonder she had said I could write my own ticket! It was plain enough now, her wanting me around.

Then I wasn't so sure.

When I peered a little closer some of them pieces didn't fit as snug as might be; some began to push up wrinkles from being squeezed in where perhaps they didn't go. Last night she'd been free of him — clean over to Tombstone. Why had she come back?

IV

I got the chin off my chest and took a sharper look around.

The sides of this canyon didn't offer much help. They was mostly rock with the rims away up so dadburned distant what sky I was able to glimpse looked bluer than Yukon ice. I could even make out a dim scatter of stars though the sun must have been well up. Down here the walls was maybe thirty foot apart with the trail antigodlin among whopping slabs and chunks cracked off through years of frosts and heat. In the lavender tinge of this shadowed passage where the horses' breaths spewed out like smoke my jacket felt rightdown good.

A man, I reckoned — if he was in good shape and was desperate enough — might be able to crawl himself up out of here, but he sure wouldn't be getting no horse up them walls.

It was things like this that had ahold of me but back of these what you might call surface activities was a hard deep core of churning thoughts. Like sniffing hounds they was dashing about with such wriggling and clamor I wondered Oakes didn't notice. *Why had she come back?*

If the girl had been a prisoner how had she managed to slip away? And why hadn't she kept on going?

I couldn't fit her into this deal.

There's been malice in what she'd said about the brand. Oakes had gone stamping off in a fury. If he'd been working for her that could figure to make sense, and I could even see if they had a good thing how he would feel some riled at her bringing me in. But if it was him she was afraid of why hadn't she said so?

The more I poked and pushed at the business the less any part of it appeared to add up. A man could get just as far toting beans, boots and buttons.

The trail took another of those sudden twists, widening some and still definitely dropping. A platter shaped valley begun to open out, looking lemon where the sun touched waving rolls of knee deep grass. There wasn't no sign of a building but there was horses scattered all through it. Must have been pretty nigh onto a hundred of them, some of the wilder ones flinging up their heads — red roans and bays and sorrels and duns, as fine looking a bunch as a feller could ask for.

"A little potbellied," Oakes grinned, "an' rough from being out, but nothing' a few feeds of grain won't cure."

"A mite light for cow work," I said, looking

over those nearest. "Them dish faced ones might have Arab in them."

"What you reckon they'll weigh?"

"Thousand, maybe. That blood bay with the snip won't top nine hundred."

Oakes fetched his glance back, nodding.

"How many you figuring on breaking?" I said.

"Many as you got time for."

I considered them again. These were short tailed horses. Taken in conjunction with the dished faces I had noticed, it seemed reasonable to suppose they were pretty well bred. "Ain't none of them acting like they're uncut studs."

"Mares an' geldin's," Oakes said, watching me. "You don't have to finish 'em. Green broke's all I want. Sooner the better."

"What's it worth?"

"Dollar a ride."

I looked at him then. I looked at him hard. The going wage for green broke — learning a bronc to start, stop and turn — was five bucks a head. Took about ten rides if you figured to get the job done.

I thought about Oakes and them eggs he'd ate. "What are they," I said, "gold plated or something?"

"All I know is I've got 'em to board. Only thing I got in 'em is what feed they've put away. You want to stomp 'em or don't you?"

"What's to prove I'll ever get paid?"

Oakes' eyes fanned around. He didn't bust into no flock of explanations. "You'll git paid," he said, "one way or another," and sent his horse jumping on up ahead.

Putting rides on broncs, like I mentioned before, ain't the easiest way in the world to make a living. That double pay looked good but a heap unlikely; and I still hadn't nothing but his word I'd collect.

I tagged along, uncommitted, to see what else he might decide to turn up.

After about ten minutes of eating his dust I come onto a hogback and, staring beyond, took in all that was left to be seen of this trough. Off there it pinched in, squeezing away through the gut of a pass that had a fence thrown across it.

The fence was cut brush stacked on end and held in place by a pair of stout ropes that had been wove through it. A girl was there, just in front, straddling one of them dish faced roans, both feet in the stirrups and a .44-77 Sharps across her lap.

That kind of gun ain't the sort you look to find in the hands of no woman. Without you know what you're doing it can lift you straight back into last week. It can knock down a buffalo at twelve hundred yards.

I couldn't guess, on that horse, how tall she might be but I could see enough, right from where I was then, to figure she wasn't no kind to write home about. She had on a man's hickory shirt, a open coat over it, her legs stuffed into a man's faded Levi's and a black flat-crowned hat chin-strapped to her jaw. I halfway thought I might be looking at Belle Starr.

It was the clothes, of course, and that authority she was packing.

Time I come up to where Oakes was talking I could see my estimate was somewhat short of doing her justice. She was in that first maturity that follows girlhood, with quick green eyes and red-gold hair, a faint suggestion of freckling across the bridge of her nose. But I'd been right about one thing. It showed in the glance she slanched across Oakes' shoulder.

"Farsom," he said, hearing me come up, "this here's my niece, Dimity Hale."

I took off my hat. "Pleasure, ma'am."

"Hello," she said, and turned back to Oakes. "I'm ready whenever you are."

Oakes' dry smile showed he got the message.

I put my hat back on, feeling about as comfortable as a bundle left on the parsonage doorstep. Oakes said, "You'll find water an' grub cached behind that red rock. I'll see that you get some more when it's needed."

He picked up his reins, kneed his horse around, the girl wheeling after him.

"Just a minute," I said. "Ain't you getting a bit ahead of yourself?"

His glance come around.

"I ain't said yet I'm hiring on for this deal."

He brought the grulla back with the lids of his eyes squeezed almost shut. "Well?"

"You got some threes and fours in this bunch. You want them broke, too?"

"I told you once. Everything you got time for."

"On the spreads I've worked they never touched anything younger than five. You're paying the same all down the line?"

"Dollar a ride."

I give him back look for look. "I'll want that in writing." He sat there so long with them dark eyes staring I was half expecting to see him go for his gun. But all he finally done was nod. "You'll git it," he grunted, and went larruping off.

The girl never did look around. Not once.

They left me with plenty of thinking to chew on. They left me so filled with notions I was about half minded to haul my freight. Then I'd remember what I had here. I'd remember Lupita. And while I stood bogged in the gulf she had give me I would find myself staring at the face of Oakes' niece and the whole sorry go-round would start up all over.

That Dimity female could sure rough a man up. She hadn't left me no more pride to set down with than a range dick could sift from a sack of shucks. Between the pair of them they had me so graveled I couldn't by God have told dung from wild honey.

I took a slow ride around. There wasn't no pens here and no stuff to make pens. There wasn't no kind of shelter if it come up a storm. Just me and them broncs and the lemon curl of last year's grass. And the goddam quiet piled up so thick you could pretty near cut it.

I rode over to the red rock and had me a look at the grub situation. About enough for a week. The cache was a box built of planks set into the ground and covered over with rusty tin. I didn't see no water, but I knew there had to be some someplace and knocked around on Oakes' buckskin till I found it, a seep oozing out of the trough's far wall, dribbling down through green slime to collect two foot deep in a slab of red sandstone that was rimmed with gray clay. This clay, darkly damp, was all chopped up with hoof tracks, some of them still wet. Wasn't no green anyplace around but that puke on the wall.

I got me a drink and let the buckskin dip his muzzle.

There was still a little shade coming down off the cliff. Once the sun climbed into the top of its swing I could see that this trough was like to heat up considerable.

It was warm already.

Getting out of my jacket I folded and tucked it into the roll with my blankets and parkers and a half mile of tarp. I was traveling light, as they say over in Texas.

While I wasn't putting all my eggs in Oakes' basket it did look to be about time I got to work. I left my rifle there too to get it out of the way and, taking down my rope, shook out a loop and looked around for a target.

The first bronc I worked was a hammer-headed moro, the only blue horse in the bunch. Then I rode two sorrels and an apron-faced bay.

It was damned sweaty business handling broncs in the open without no chute or squeeze or pen or nothing to cramp a horse down to. Time I got off that bay I was ready for a rest.

When I'd cooled off some I got me a drink. The more I thought about the wages Oakes had offered the less likely it seemed that I would ever collect them.

The whole deal smelled. All the way back to where I'd met up with Lupita. Even the way I had been sucked into this.

And yet there wasn't a thing a man could rightly put his finger on. Nothing, I mean, that mightn't be made to appear perfectly reasonable. Even Oakes out here plumb alone with two fillies. But the stink persisted, and smelled like trouble — big trouble.

Take this caballado, for instance. One horse may look pretty much like another, but not to a man who'd punched cows for a living. There is as much difference in horses as there is in people. Really top horses are about as scarce as top hands, the percentage shaking down to about one in twenty. Yet this bunch Oakes had here, near as I could tell from looking, wouldn't number probably more than a dozen that shaped up below being mighty fine animals. Clean limbed, close coupled, sound of wind and long on bottom. For size, for muscling, for the way they handled themselves and stood, there wasn't a jughead in the lot.

That just wasn't natural. A kid could have told you this bunch was hand picked. Small hoofed, thin legged, bright eyed — every one of them. And every last one of them packing the same brand.

I got up off my heels and stepped back into leather. The buckskin whickered, shaking the flies away from his face. The shadows was building out from the wall; we had about three hours left to go. My appetite was beginning to catch up with me but I reckoned I could maybe top off a couple more. Shaking out my loop I eased in on a roan. We had quite a chase with him ducking and wheeling back and forth through the pack before I could get a clear chance. He stopped like he was shot when that rope snapped around him. Smart. The whole bunch was. They'd been roped at before.

But they hadn't been ridden. It was fight all the way. That bronc had more tricks than a dog has fleas. He stood like a stone while I was cinching the rig on — I hauled his head around and swung up. Then he jumped sideways, dropped his bill and started pitching. He sunfished and twisted, swapped ends and pump-handled. He tried to run out from under me. When he finally give up I couldn't of lasted another jump.

I cuffed him around for another few minutes, yanking the sonofabitch this way and that. He savvied all right, acting meeker than a kitten. I got off him then while he knew who was boss.

We scowled at each other and I couldn't help laughing. You could almost see the notions wheel through his head.

Don't let nobody tell you a horse has no humor.

I pulled off hackamore and kack and slapped his lathered rump. He threw up his tail and went squealing away to join the others.

He had sure took it out of me.

V

I was up the next morning at first crack of light, putting together a breakfast over a fire of dried horse apples. I hadn't got much rest, though sleeping on the ground come just as natural as breathing. I was stiff and filled with groans from that jouncing but it was the things in my head that had made me so twisty.

That Squabble O brand Lupita had called 'Cyclops' was the only iron these broncs was marked with, and I'd have bet any chance I had of collecting it had come out of Mexico. Probably come in a hurry from some big holding like Valdepeñas or the hacienda at Nacozari. Stolen, of course. Run up this smuggler's trail and left with Oakes for board and breaking. It wouldn't make no difference that I hadn't stole them if some of those long-eared sons of generals with braid all over come up here and found them.

If they'd of been took recent there'd have been more sign. They'd been here long enough anyway to put on pot bellies from eating cured grass.

Despite the number of things I didn't like about this deal it was still a fair setup for a man hunting cover — no getting away from that. Or from thinking of those two females living under one roof alone with Fred Oakes and whatever he was up to.

I was scrubbing sand in the skillet — it and a bent fork being the only eating tools I'd found — when I remembered Oakes asking if I was kin to Curly Bill. What I wondered, had prompted that notion? It wasn't the sort of question a man would ordinary ask.

Curly Bill, if you don't know it, was about as rough as they'd come in this country. A Texican. A loud-laughing clown with black hair and smith's shoulders, quick on the shoot and with no more scruples than you'd find in a snake. Dead now, they said, killed by Wyatt Earp someplace in the brush; but a little bit back, when I'd been riling John Chisum on behalf of Murphy-Dolan, Curly Bill in this region had been the kingpin bandido and had rode sometimes with forty men at his back.

No kind of guy to stamp your boot and yell boo! at. All the owlhoots at this end of the catclaw had owed some manner of allegiance to him, and he had sure cut a swath with his stealing and shooting. He'd took cattle wholesale from both sides of the line. He'd killed a mort of smugglers and sacked several towns, including Matamoras. John Bingo rode with him and the Clantons and McLowerys. He run off Army horses but there was nothing cheap about him. He come and went at his own sweet will. He'd even dabbled in politics, voting a batch of chickens and pigs and, by God, got away with it.

Now here was Fred Oakes wanting to know first pop out of the box if I was kin to him.

I chucked the pan back into the grub box, caught up my bridle and went after the buckskin. I'd left him hobbled for safe keeping so I didn't have to tromp more than a mile to come up with him. I fetched him in and put my rig on, kneed the wind out of his gut and took up the slack. I rode him across and let him wet his whistle. Wrapping a knee round the horn then I got out Durham and papers and twisted up a smoke while I looked the outfit over.

I didn't spot nothing I hadn't seen before.

The sun was beginning to gild the far wall. The air was sweet with the smells of grass and horses and the sky overhead was a clean bright blue. About as peaceful a view as a feller could ask. The things on my mind didn't look so dark now. There was probably nothing wrong with Oakes a fuller acquaintance wouldn't set straight.

I shook out my loop and got to work.

Three days slipped by, the weather staying clear, the nights continuing cool and the grub getting lower in the red rock cache. The job progressed, moving a little faster now that I'd got in the swing of it.

Nineteen of Oakes' broncs had a good work behind them and I was topping the twentieth about the middle of the morning when some of them others set up a racket of nickering.

I couldn't catch me no look. The clown between my knees was trying to drive all the bones straight up through my noggin. When he finally jumped off the dime and took to weaving I had all I could do to keep from losing the leathers. I thought for sure my head would tear off. It was like some bastard had the back of my belt and was shaking me same as a wrung-out bar rag.

Then the damn bronc stuck his bill in the ground. While my teeth was shifting he slatted his sails and hopped for mama.

I went through the air. I come down, throwing up dust like a plow with my chin, all spraddled out and piling up in a heap.

When I finally got my face pulled clear it felt like half my joints was unhinged. Probably looked that way too if you could seen me trying to get up out of it. I didn't hardly know one end from the other.

I'd forgot about the nickering. Alls I could hear was this roarin like a big wind rushing through me. All I could see was a whirling of ground, yellow grass, sky and horses.

Then they flopped into place. I heard the laugh and, twisting my head, seen her settin there shaking like what I had done was the funniest ever — Oakes' sorrel-topped niece, still in pants and still lugging that chunk of artillery.

"You'll wet your britches," I said, "an' I hope you do!"

It wasn't no way to talk to a lady. I didn't give a whoop if she whirled straight around and went back to Oakes with it. I looked for her to.

Her cheeks fired up but all she done was set there. She didn't look furious or even insulted, nor was she ignoring me like she had when her uncle was around.

She suddenly chuckled. "You git hurt?"

I reckon I did look pretty foolish. "Generally," I said, "I pass the hat about now," and watched to see if it would fetch back the grin.

"Hat?" she said.

I limped over and fished it out of a pear clump. "Just a old Farsom saying. How long you been with your uncle?"

She pushed a dangle of hair from her face and continued to stare while I picked out the stickers. A queer one, all right. You might have reckoned by her stare I had two heads or a tail, maybe. "The old man," I said, wanting to shake her, "Fred Oakes."

"Oh. I've always been here . . . pretty near, anyway. He isn't my uncle — not really."

I must of looked blank. "Fred found me," she said. "Near some burnt wagons. I guess I wasn't much bigger'n a minute."

It was my turn to stare. "Mean he give you a home? Raised you up?" It sure didn't fit my picture of Fred Oakes.

Her green eyes, widening, darkened. "He

wants you back at the house."

"What for? And where's that grub he was supposed to send out?"

She did smile then, somewhat meager-like and doubtful. She said, and it was like Fred Oakes himself talking, "I'm not in the business of answering questions. You better climb back on that bronc or you never will be able to do anything with him."

Didn't help my temper none to be reminded. I got my rope and went after him.

I should have known better than to think I could ever get near enough on foot. Feeling like a fool I had to come back after the buckskin and get up on him bareback.

Time I caught the bronc and got back in the saddle Dimity Hale was halfway to the cliffs. This was a four-year-old and some set up with himself for having dumped me. He tried to fling me off again as soon as I got on him. Then he reached around to bite off my leg.

I worked him over with hat and spurs. The more he bucked the worse I used him. He was tough as a white oak and twice as ornery as any mule. I begun to wonder if I was going to make it.

When he quit the girl was clean out of sight.

I was mightily tempted to ignore Oakes' summons. My job, as laid out, was to put rides on these horses; I wasn't being paid to run errands for Oakes. But he had sent the girl after me. Maybe he'd changed his mind about the deal. I looked around for the buckskin, found he'd gone frisking off with a bunch of them others. Swearing, I put the hooks to the bronc.

He took off like a bat out of Carlsbad. I cuffed him with my hat and got him pointed at the cliffs where they come together in that trail the girl had come in by. He must of figured to run out from under me. He had plenty of speed, I'll say that for him.

The girl was waiting just beyond the first bend. It was plain she didn't much approve of what she saw. "What are you tryin' to do — kill him?"

"I thought you was in a hurry," I said.

She give me another of them long cool looks and without saying anything started her horse on past. I put out a fist and grabbed her arm and the snout of that Sharps rammed me hard in the belly.

I let out a grunt. I let go of her, too. Her eyes looked green as two pieces of glass.

"When I want to be pawed I'll tell you," she said. "Now get on back to the ranch like Fred told you."

There didn't seem to be much else I could do, not with that rifle staring down my throat.

My return to Silver Spring was done a heap quicker than the way I had left, but it wasn't no ride I hanker to look back on. I didn't have much time for thinking. Twice the damn bronc tried to take off a leg by scraping me into the sides of the walls.

By the grace of good luck most of the hide he took off was his own, but that didn't keep him content for long. He tried a dozen times to get his teeth into me and every time he made his move I put another lump on his jaw. I had to watch him all the way, every minute, with the chances odds-on that before he got through he would pile me up in spite of all hell.

He had lather all over by the time we got in. You'd of thought, the way he was using up energy, he'd have been plumb docile. He was wet as a cow's tongue but when I swung off damned if he didn't try to slam a hoof into me. I jumped for the porch with the halter shank, sloshed it twice around a post and left him there tied solid. I knew one thing for sure: he had all the ride I aimed to put on him!

I wiped the blood off my lip and sung out. When nobody answered I put a fist to the door.

"You don't have to break it down," Lupita called. "Come on in and take the weight off your feet."

I pushed open the door. She was over by the cupboard putting dishes away, but the first thing I seen was this guy with the gun. He had it pointed straight at me, teeth bared, the eyes looking like burnt holes in his face.

VI

He was backed against a wall, a stringy wisp of a feller with a weak-chinned jaw, fright stretching the skin tight as vellum across the bones of his skull beneath its thatch of red hair. The gun — a gambler's pepperbox — begun waggling in his fist like the tail of a nervous cat.

Lupita screamed. "Not him — you fool! That's Farsom, Jake's hired hand!"

Indecision spread like cracks through his stare but the revolver's yawing focus never quit my shape till Fred Oakes, sounding disgusted, growled, "For Chrissake, Brace, git aholt of yerself." Only then did its muzzle grudgingly dip toward the floor.

My tongue rasped over two mighty dry lips. The nearness of it put claws in my stomach. A kind of wild fury begun to pound through but, before I could scrape up enough spit to cuss, a board someplace retched out a thin wheeze. In a quiet, thick-carpeted with unspoken thoughts, a second guy come limping in from the back.

Younger, this one, awkwardly unsure in his

patched hand-me-downs and runover boots. Not more, I put him, than maybe sixteen, though big for his age. Tow hair showed under his hat's floppy brim, milky eyes, the merest nubbin of a nose. His pants was kept up by a twist of frayed rope. Between pants and shirt was wedged the notched butt of a nickel-plated pistol.

With him at my right and the redhead off to the plumb farthest left of where I might keep peeled eyes on the both of them it didn't seem no time to be flapping my jaw. Particular after I got a squint at Fred Oakes.

He looked like a man coming off a bad drunk.

Could have been the way that light struck across him pouring off the rocks. He kept rubbing together his goddam teeth the way a wormy cow might do and breathing like he'd just run a full four-forty.

He clamped a hand to the table and got out of his chair like it was a hard thing to do. He took time then to swaller.

"Farsom —" he said, and cleared the squeaks from his throat. "Farsom, these here is friends from over the mountain. Cort Brace," he said, jerking his chin at the pepper-box, "an' Alamagordo. Boys . . . He grabbed for more breath with his eyes swiveling round like two bats in the buckbrush, "have yerselfs a good look at my pardner, Flick Farsom."

I could cheerfully have knocked the teeth down his neck. The lie was bad enough; they weren't his friends, and, more to the point, I wasn't his partner. But the worst was putting that handle to my name. He hadn't no call at all to do that.

I never looked at the kid. Cort Brace — the redhead — in black coat and grimy linen stood froze to his pepper-box stiff as a gatepost. Nothing come through the gray cant of that stare.

For me, nothing had to. It went without saying if he'd been around at all he would know who Flick Farsom was, the part I had played in that Lincoln County shoot-out.

I took a wrap around my temper.

The arrival of this pair had certainly upset Oakes. He looked to have aged ten years since leaving me out on that grass, though I couldn't see anything about a fool kid or this rablity tinhorn to put his wind up.

Calling him a liar wouldn't help any. It looked like I'd better string along for a spell till I could see where the play was headed. I wondered if these jaspers had come about the horses.

Lupita, with a sniff, went off to the kitchen.

Brace's hands when I looked back at him was empty. His glance slid away and with the barest of nods he went over to a window and stood there staring out.

The kid never give me that much even. Still glowering at Oakes he flopped into a chair. "I don't know why you had to drag him —"

"I'll do the talkin'," Brace said. "You want to

make yourself useful go out an' walk that horse you'll find tied to the porch."

The kid didn't look like he was figuring to go anywhere, but he got up when Brace turned and went grumbling out. I pulled the chair against the wall and tipped back in it, crossing my arms. Oakes didn't seem in much of a hurry to get at whatever it was he had wanted with me. Maybe all he'd wanted was to give these sports a chance to find out he wasn't quite alone.

I said to the gambler, "What's your interest in this outfit?"

They didn't either of them like it. Brace, at least, kept the scowls off his face. "I expect," he said with a sly grin for Oakes, "I'm what you might call another of Fred's 'pardners'."

Oakes liked that even less by the look. I could hear Lupita moving around in the kitchen.

A man would of had to been deaf, dumb and blind not to feel the things that was poking their heads up. I would stick, I reckoned, till I got some chuck in me, then pick up the dun and roll my cotton. Two girls and Fred and now this pair all holed up together was no kind of deal for any gent who aimed to put wrinkles on his horns.

Brace pulled out a chair and, straddling it, said, "Whatever happened to that girl you had here, Fred — the one called you 'uncle'?"

Oakes pushed around the chaw in his mouth. "You'll find her, like enough, if you look."

"Well, now, I might just do that," Brace smiled, and got up. "That your horse outside, Farsom?"

"Belongs to the outfit."

"You object if I borry him?"

"Help yourself."

But, soon as he went out, I said Oakes, "You think that's smart? Putting him onto that girl?"

He stepped over to the window, come hotfooting back. "Listen," he said, "I'll make this right —"

"Don't waste your breath. Soon's I put a few beans in the boiler I'm cuttin' my stick. What about the girl?"

He grabbed my arm. "You can't go now — not while I got that pair on my shirttail!"

I eyed him, quiet. "I can go any time I make up my mind to." I threw off his hand. I got out of the chair.

"God damn it," Oakes snarled, "will you listen a minute! Them sonsabithches is fixin' to *kill* me."

"You should of thought about that before you run off their horses."

"Horses?" Oakes cursed. "Them goddamn broncs ain't got nothin' to —"

"Neither have I. Ain't aimin' to, either."

From down wind someplace come a flutter of hoof sound. Oakes, with his eyes looking big as slop buckets, whirled and run from the house.

Lupita come from the kitchen. "Flick . . . Fred's right! That pair mean to kill him before —"

"Guys don't go round killing other guys for nothing."

She didn't look half so cuddly as she had. She was scairt, all right. You could see it in her stare, the way her breath jumped. "What do you figure I can do?" I said, watching her.

"You got to keep those fools from killing Jake."

I said, "You mean Fred, don't you?"

She'd been excited, of course. Her nod acknowledged it. "I won't lie to you, Flick. His real name's Gauze — he was in on those Skeleton Canyon massacres. I was afraid if I told you you wouldn't come out."

There ain't nothing like making a clean breast of things for disarming a man if you got the right shape for it. I could pretty near hear the wheels going round behind that little-girl look she'd dug up for me.

Jake Gauze. Well, it figured. One of Curly Bill's bunch. I didn't wonder he'd been riled when she come dragging me in.

The red lips grinned. "Didn't I tell you," she laughed, "you could write your own ticket?"

Maybe my look wasn't bright as it should of been. She said, coming nearer, "It wasn't Jake wanted you, it was *me*," and held her mouth up.

"Reckon you better spell that out."

The black eyes blazed. "Lupita don' throw herself at *any* man, hombre!"

A guy could believe that. With them lumps of warm flesh joggling around like ripe melons she didn't look to need to; but a feller would of had to been dumber than me. . . . I backed off for more air.

I could feel the old Adam climbing through my blood. It was plain what she was offering. Question was *why?*

She come right up against me and I never moved a finger.

Breath whistled out of her. "What are you — a mouse!"

"A man could get hurt reachin' for something like that," I said, hot around the collar.

She spun away from me in scorn, flouncing over to a window looking out across the porch. Almost at once she put her back to it, still angry but seeming someway desperate. "You've got to stay."

"Give me one good reason."

She said, "Don't you feel like you owe him anything!"

"He's had good measure from what grub I've et."

"You're impossible!" she blazed. Then her eyes winnowed down. "Would you stay for a sixth?"

"A sixth of what?"

Fred Oakes come in. Before she could move he'd cuffed her hard across the face, force enough in it to send her reeling against the wall. "You goddam slut!"

Seldom have I seen such fury in a man. He fetched his stare around to me. "No matter what she told you them horses ain't in this — you're not gettin' a one of 'em! Understand?"

I felt like telling him what he could do with

them horses. Then I got hold of myself. A man could look pretty foolish trading insults with a loony.

"Never mind," I said. "I'm gettin' out."

Still watching me, he scraped the back of a hand across his cheeks. "I hope you brought your walkin' shoes."

"What's that supposed to mean?"

"Means we're afoot. Goddamn kid run all the ponies outa that pen. Choused 'em to hell an' gone off down the canyon!"

VII

He watched me with a slippery grin, peering from the door when I stepped out to have a look for myself. I went far enough to know this wasn't no bluff he'd put up.

It appeared I was pretty well stuck with this deal; they had run off my dun along with the rest. Remembering the hours it had took to get here I wasn't even about to put hope in a shank's mare. If there'd been nothing else, saddle boots plain wasn't built for hiking.

Which ain't to say I'd give up by a jugful.

I went back to the house.

Oakes or Gauze or whatever his name was was still in the doorway picking his teeth with a sharpened match. He turned and went in and come out with a chair. He put his butt into it cool as you please and, tilting back, propped his legs up. That grin had again got the lips off his teeth.

I hunkered down by a post. He wasn't looking at me but off towards them rocks masking the mouth of the canyon where he'd shown me the bones he'd said had come from dead smugglers.

If this was Jake Gauze it was a cinch he'd helped kill them.

I considered him slanchways, wondering what he'd found to be tickled at. Not ten minutes back he'd been so wild and mixed up he'd took his hand to the girl and knocked her half silly, and all on account of he had jumped to the notion she'd been about to deal me a share in that bronc pool. Before that he'd been half out of his pants in the conviction that that pair had come here to murder him. Lupita apparently had thought so too, yet there he sat as smug and complacent as a frog on a lily pad waiting for flies.

Either he hadn't been scairt — but that didn't make sense. He'd been scairt, right enough. He'd come back from the corrals mad as a drunk squaw, howling them two had put us afoot. In a towering rage he'd lit into her. Between that business and this grin on his mug was just a handful of grumbles. Was it something he'd got out of her while I'd been gone? Or was the damn fool chuckling because I was stuck here?

A little time slipped away, maybe a couple or three minutes.

Oakes hitched over on one hip. "How you doin' out there?" He made it sound real chummy. "Shapin' up pretty good are they?"

"Soon's I can get me a horse, I'm clearing out," I said.

"I wouldn't count too much on it," he said, sounding smug again. "That tinhorn, Brace, ain't no amachoor, you know."

"He ain't no horse breaker, either."

Oakes peered at me, scowling, not getting it. I jerked my jaw at the rocks. "Ain't that him on the saddle?"

The legs of Oakes' chair hit the floor with a thump, but he didn't get out of it. Like me he just stared, holding silent. Then he laughed.

It was something to see, if you like watching cripples. That old pepperbox wasn't in sight at the moment and not much of Brace, belly down like he was. The kid, with the chin plumb nudging his brisket and the reins of Oakes' horse hoisted over one shoulder, looked to be furnishing most of the power for this travel, sloggin along on his runover boots and apparently not caring if school kept or not.

"Have a accident, boys?" I called out, cheerful.

The kid never lifted his eyes off the trail, never paused, swerved or nothing, but Brace quit groaning long enough to curse.

They come into the yard and hauled up by the porch. We could see then what ailed him. He was a sure enough mess. The shirt was half out of the back of his pants and from shoulder blades down to the backs of his knees he was practically plastered with silverspined cholla.

"Just goes to show," I said, "what can happen to a gent that takes another feller's horse."

Oakes had been having himself a real time admiring that slob with all the cactus stuck in him. Now he broke it off short, all the breath wheezing out of him. It was a toss-up which looked the meanest, him or that kid.

Brace said, "You going to for Chrissake stan' there all day?"

The kid flung down the reins. "Yeah," I said, "you better ease him off."

I didn't notice much wrong with Brace's talking talent except his remarks run to pretty lurid language. Alamagordo looked meaner than a new-sheared sheep. "C'mon," he snarled, "git down here an' give me a hand!"

Oakes stayed where he was, and me with him.

I thought for a minute the kid was going to go for his pistol he was so goddam mad. But Lupita come out and, ignoring the both of us, tossed him a pair of fence cutting tools. "Try these."

Even with them pliers — Brace alternately howling and swearing — the kid took pretty near a plum half hour to get enough room cleared for hand holds. He worked till the light got too poor to see by, and then with the tinhorn folded over his shoulder staggered onto the porch. Brace swearing a blue streak what time he wasn't groaning.

The girl held the door. "Put him in that back bedroom." She followed them in.

I looked at Oakes. "What have they got on you?"

He forted himself up behind that scraggle of whiskers, hunching there like he was glued to the chair.

I got out my pipe. Trying the bowl with my thumb I put the fire to it while I tried to decide if

I should take Oakes' horse. It was a powerful temptation. I was pulled two ways, knowing I'd probably never get a better chance. I could take care of Oakes — a tap from my gun barrel would hold him quiet, but what about them two fillies? Same thing must have been in Oakes' head. He got up sudden and, stepping out of reach, said, "I'll put up that horse," and was off the steps before I got my legs under me.

Probably just as well. I don't reckon I'd of got far, worrying over them females. They weren't my lookout but after seeing the way he had swung on Lupita I wouldn't of felt right just up and going off.

Something else got to chewing my tender disposition. What if Oakes, out of sight, piled into that saddle and kept straight on?

I was minded to go after him. Fact is I was on my way when this other notion hit and brought me, scowling, to a standstill.

Might be best to let him do it. From what I'd seen it appeared a heap likely if he yanked his picket pin Brace and that kid would be right on his tail. No trouble at all then for me to grab a horse; and if the girls wanted to leave — I never doubted *that* part, I could mount them up too.

Lupita come out again. "Flick — is that you?"

She looked tall against the lights. She was a damn attractive woman.

I went back. "He's took off," I said, "to put up his grulla. If his feet's cold enough he may skeedadle and you'll be rid of him."

"Flick — you've got to stop him!"

I guess the lights showed my astonishment. She said with the words tumbling over each other, "I know it sounds crazy but he mustn't. . . . Call it a woman's intuition. Something in here —" She clamped a hand over her bosom. "You've got to stop him!"

"Well . . . I thought you didn't want him killed?"

"Hurry!" she cried. "We can't let him get away!"

So I went peltin towards the corrals, all mixed up in my head but doing her bidding, distrusting the woman but infected by her urgency. She certainly knew Oakes better than I did. If she wanted him around . . .

I didn't, as it turned out, have to go at all. I was busting around the last of them rocks when his voice come against me like the rasp of a saw. "Whoa up! Strike a light!"

"Farsom," I told him, feeling ringy and foolish.

"Figures," he said, coming up with a chuckle. "Reckon you thought I'd took out."

I wondered if he'd seen the gun in my fist.

"Well, no harm done." He patted my shoulder, turned me back towards the house. "You don't want to take all my wife says fer gospel."

I must of choked hard enough to be heard clean to Roswell. I turned cold and then hot, the heat swirling over me, remembering the way she'd took hold of her bosom.

Oakes nudged me into motion. "She's wropped smarter men than you round her finger. Old game with her, playin' boys fer suckers."

We tramped on in silence.

I was thankful for the dark and filled with a mighty burning.

"You'll git over it," Oakes said. "Once bit, twice shy. A good think to remember."

I was remembering plenty.

He didn't say no more till we come into the lights. Then, kind of under his breath, he said, "You want to play this smart, let her think you stopped me. Mebbe, given enough rope, she'll tip her hand."

"If she's that kind —"

"They broke the mold, after her. Wouldn't surprise me none if it turns out she sent fer — Here, let me go ahead. You keep right behind me."

I thought at first she'd gone inside but she was still there, waiting, backed into the shadows between two windows.

Oakes, ignoring her, went on in. I'd of done the same but her hand, snakin' out, latched onto my arm. "Flick —" She drew me into the shadows. I could feel her breath on my cheek. She said, "Was he?"

"He didn't quite make it."

She said softly, "Thanks," and hugged my arm. "I'll make it up to you." She pushed me toward the door.

The perfidy of her nearly turned my guts. But for her I might have ridden out of this mess. In the Bible they had a name for her kind.

I shoved her out of my thoughts. She went into the kitchen. I looked over at Oakes. "Think he'll live through it?"

Oakes was sprawled in a chair with a glass in his fist. Looked like his mind was a hundred miles away. He was a hard man to like but I could almost feel sorry for him, being tied up to a dame like that.

The door to the back bedroom was shut but you could hear the occasional skreak of a bed-spring through the interminable murmur of Brace's moans and mumblings. Alamagordo said presently, sounding fed up, "Either hold still, by Gawd, or pick the rest out yourself!"

I went back to the porch and dug out my pipe, but the smoke was no good. I kept thinking about Lupita, about her lying eyes and her lying red mouth and calling myself twenty kinds of a fool. But supposing, I thought, it had been him that lied? that she wasn't his wife!

I got up and knocked out my pipe. She was probably what he had called her; all my experience endorsed it and there had been real conviction in the sound of Oakes' voice.

Jake Gauze she had named him, a fly-by-night vulture; but all I had was her word for it, a woman I'd come onto in a Tombstone deadfall, a harpy who preyed on a man's natural feelings to entangle me in this damned web of hate and treachery.

I grinned, a little sheepish. I guessed that was piling it on pretty thick. From what I had heard of him, if Oakes was Jake Gauze he could probably make out to take care of himself.

I got to pawing around. It was astonishing how little I was able to turn up, aside from the fact the man had had a bad name. He'd been with Curly Bill — or certainly had been named with him, Old Man Clanton, Ike and Billy Clanton, Tom and Frank McLowery, John Ringo, Jim Hughes, Joe Hill, Rattlesnake Bill, Charlie Thomas and Charlie Snow, in that canyon massacre that had — sometime in July of '81 — wiped out Don Miguel Garcia and his smuggler train, only one 'handsome stripling' getting away to tell of it. Loot from this foray was held at seventy-five thousand in Mexican silver. A month or so later the gang had gotten wind of another and even bigger expedition bound for Tucson by way of that trail. When Jim Hughes arrived Curly Bill was in Charleston. With no time to fiddle around getting word to him, Hughes set the stage himself, rigging an ambush with the outlaws over ninety thousand in Mexican money plus thirty-nine bars of very solid gold. Gauze was figured to have been in on this, too. It was, even by repute, the only other dido with which I could connect him.

Now another idea got hold of me.

When Oakes had come in like the wrath of God to send Lupita banging into that wall, I had figured it was because he'd reckoned she was cutting me in for a sixth of them horses. Could have been jealous rage. Or he could have jumped to some conclusion that had nothing to do with her or them broncs — like maybe his cut of the swag from them killings. If he still had it.

I had to admit this didn't look a heap likely.

Outlaw money is quick to the pocket and, generally speaking, even faster spent. Plenty figured they would pile up a stake but few of them done it; not even Jack Ketcham. John Chisum that I had quit for Murphy-Dolan had taken a mort of cattle out of Texas but he probably couldn't rub three dimes together now. Jesse James had died strapped, Cole Younger and Quantrill likewise. Old man Clanton — and he had been a shrewd devil, had been pretty near stony when a bushwhacker bullet come along with his name.

Still, it didn't look reasonable when a man stood off for Oakes to have got in such a sodpawing fury over a jag of broncs he'd said himself didn't belong to him. If a man had put enough trust in his wife — but Oakes hadn't talked like he put any at all in her.

I went on in to find him still in his chair. His eyes looked so glassy I thought — remembering that tumbler — he had got himself plastered, but he come out of it hearing me and, scowling, made some attempt to pull himself together. Twisting his head he bellered, "What the goddam hell have you done with the grub!"

From the region of the stove there came a

racket of pots and pans; she'd been keeping it warm, apparently, waiting for Brace and the kid to come in. She must of had it ready because she come right in with it — two platters of sow belly and half a kettle of ham hocks and beans. "Pull up a chair," Oakes growled, and done likewise. By the time we were settled she was back with the java, pouring the mugs and darting looks at Oakes slanchways.

He shoved out an arm when she turned back to the stove. "By God, fer once you'll eat with me!" She stood with hands gripped together, dark eyes on him, nervous. "But Fred . . . we've got guests. . . ."

"*I* never ast 'em here! Now get onto that bench and put some grub on yer plate."

Smiling stiffly she climbed over it and got her legs out of sight. I reckon she was furious but if she was it didn't show. Strain, pulling her skin tight, was the only difference noticeable, that and the fact she spoke only when talked at. Oakes chewed noisily, shoveling food to his face as though he'd news a bad famine was just around the corner.

Mostly Lupita kept her eyes on her plate. Once when she looked up I winked. "Brace say how he come to pick up that cactus?"

She didn't wink back but said civilly enough that, according to Alamagordo, they'd run onto Dimity Hale in one of the canyon's narrower twists, that before either one of them could open their mouths she'd whipped up that Sharps and loosed a blue whistler. All that saved Brace was the brass horn of my saddle. The bronc — with that blast and the slug's shock of impact — had stuck his bill in the ground and heaved Brace like a flap-jack into a five-foot clump of spined cholla.

This account of Brace's misadventures appeared to have put Oakes in somewhat better fettle. His belly shook. "That Dimity!" he said with every evidence of admiration, the fervence of which was not lost upon Lupita.

He looked around to grin at me.

"Guess you reckoned old Fred a pretty sorry bastard sendin' two like them off to badger that girl, but I knowed what I was doin'. She coulda killed Brace jest as easy. Matter of fact," he scowled, "I figgered she would — was kinda hopin' she'd ventilate the both of 'em."

He had certainly give me something to remember. I hid my ire behind a lift of java, but one thing was plain as the hump on a camel. Any jasper as twisty as that would bear watching.

When I glanced up again his look was filled with listening.

Took another couple heartbeats before I picked up myself the faint *clop clop* of a walking horse that finally whittled to a stop someplace out beyond the porch. From Oakes' frozen look I knew it wasn't Dimity.

He had both hands spread flat against the top of the table.

VIII

He looked like a gopher about to pop in its hole.

A door, creaking open, sounded raucous as the top being pried off a coffin. A thump of feet come towards us. The gambler hove into sight, dethorned, sponged off and swelled up in his clothes with the courage he'd apparently augmented from a bottle.

He smelt like Saturday night at Big Emma's. His glance, darting over our faces, bugged a little as he sniffed at the stillness. With his nose coming up like a rabbit's he stopped so short the kid, limping after, rammed into him.

Brace, shoving the kid off his elbow, in the fog of his libations tried on a grin for size. "Well!" he exclaimed, blearily blinking. "You can't raise a ghost without you grab hol' of han's."

"Ghost . . ." Lupita stiffened. In the whitness of her cheeks the staring eyes was black as coals. "What ghost?"

So choked was her voice I had to guess at the words.

The crazy tinhorn whacked his thigh. "The

ghost of Curly Bill!" he chortled, and flung back his head in a gurgle of guffaws.

Something almost frightening got into the feel of the thickening quiet. Across it come a hail from the dark — more a flutterous whisper it sounded to me. "Hallo-o-o the house!"

Thin as a thread, horribly bloating, the call crept and curled through that jumpety hush. Then the question, "Someone call me?"

You'd of swore Oakes had petrified. Not a breath moved in nor out of him.

Leather squealed under shifted weight. Come a tinkle of spur chains, feet slapping ground, inescapably nearer. These come after the Voice, one by one, to circle and join in their romp of the room.

Sweat stood out on Oakes' lip like rain.

Feet stomped across the porch, knuckles thumped. "You all dead in there?"

Again Oakes astonished me. "Come in, Bill," he growled, pushing up from his chair.

Lupita clutched at her throat.

The man who came in was a swaggering dandy with a fierce black mustache and a good-natured grin. A handsome devil with a real air about him.

There was gloves on his hands. While he was peeling them I took a sharp look. Brown pants he wore over the tops of bright boots and a brown frock coat open all the way down. A blue cravat bound the stand-up collar and there was the carriage of him, too, his importance an observable quality as plain to grasp — as unquestionably his, as the feet inside those fine Justin boots.

A wine colored weskit embroidered in yellow was tight buttoned over his chest, with a length of gold cable swung from pocket to pocket above the soft blaze of a turkey red sash. One other item no eye would of missed was two bone-handled sixshooters pouched in brown leathers, strapped so they held back the skirts of his coat.

He said, "Your servant, ma'am," with a whimsical grin, his bow of an elegance not to be matched except by the charm of some Mex hacendado. With his hundred-dollar hat tucked under his arm he shut out the night and come back to us looking as completely at ease as if he'd been made blood brother to everyone.

I wondered how many of this outfit knew him. Oakes sure enough. Probably Lupita — though she seemed, I thought, somewhat less than delighted. One thing I'd have bet: he was *not* Curly Bill. He had the mustache, and more guts than John Chisum who could stare down a mountain cat, but his hair didn't have as much curl as a Injun's — his whole build was different.

He tossed the hat carelessly not two foot from the gambler who jumped back in such alarm I had to grin in spite of myself.

Every move this hombre made was done with a sort of flourish. Put me in mind of one of them play-acting fellers. His voice was strong and deep as a snake-oil peddler's and, just now with his stare swiveling back to Oakes, so bland new butter wouldn't melt in his mouth.

"Come, come, good host. Make me known to your friends."

Something more felt than seen passed between them — nothing a guy could put a handle to.

Oakes' sigh was the kind that comes out of old dogs. "You know my wife. . . ."

"Know that one, too. Pink Cort Brace." The feller's grin skewered the tinhorn with a contempt so plain you could pretty near taste it. "Sort of figured he'd probably put in here for water."

Whatever had brought these people together — and never for a minute did I think such a bunch had just happened to turn up, he was giving the gambler a chance to get out. Maybe it wasn't the whole shape of his meaning, but this much stood out public as paint.

Seemed like Brace thought so too, the way he colored.

Oakes, with his lip skun back a little, nodded. "Gent to the left there's my pardner, Farsom — 'Flick' they called him in the Seven Rivers country. Kid come with Pink." Oakes' stare cut around. "Boys," he said on an upswing of breath, "meet Bill Ivory," and sat abruptly down.

The man peered at him, concerned. "You ailin'?"

"Nothin'," Oakes grumbled, "I can't make out to put up with."

Ivory's eyes let go of him and, ignoring the kid, wiped a look over me. "You buying into this?"

"Does it make any difference?"

His cold grin flashed. He took his look at the girl. "And how are you, Mrs. Oakes?"

"Feeling pretty fair till you walked in."

Ivory chuckled. "What I've always liked about you. Straight as an arrow, sharp as cut glass." He dropped a hip on the table, little imps of mischief jumping up and down behind the glint of that glance. "Any luck?"

She flounced off to the kitchen with a wriggle and a scowl, but not before I'd seen the fury that was in her.

"Be a cruel waste to have a woman like that folded over her sewin' like a hog with its throat slit." Above the twist of his grin Ivory's bold look shuttled across the blobs of our faces. It didn't seem like to me he was more than half funning. "By the way," he called after her, "where-at's that filly you been fetchin' up for Red? Filled out any, has she?"

Lupita said, cool enough, "Better ask Pink. Way I heard, she ran him into a cactus."

Color plowed into Brace's face. Bill Ivory laughed but Oakes appeared deaf as a gatepost. Ivory winked. "What does a feller have to do to get fed here?"

"He has to be around," Lupita spat, "when its ready!"

Brace muttered, "Reckon I'll turn in," and turned for the hall.

"Door you're hunting's over yonder," Ivory motioned. "Better take a blanket. Gets rightdown chilly up here before morning."

The kid, who had got up to follow, looked around with a scowl but Brace kept going.

He was nearly to the hall when Ivory said real soft, "I'm taking that room myself. Steer away from it."

Brace, snarling, come around and, yanking open the door, stomped off across the porch so mad you could pretty near hear his teeth crack. Alamagordo, looking puckered around the edges, limped along in his wake.

Ivory stepped through after them and, just out of sight, called, "You there, kid! Put that horse in the corral. Rub him down good and see that he's grained. When you get that done I want some hay forked to him."

He stepped back in and closed the door.

I expect it was pretty plain what I thought. Under his mustache I seen the gleam of Ivory's teeth. "You can't bake a cake without you break a few eggs."

I could of said several things, they was right on my tongue. But how he treated that kid wasn't no skin off my butt.

Oakes, across the room, was deep sunk in his rocker — sunk, by the look of him, in more ways than one. Ivory, considering him, scooped up his hat. He said towards the kitchen, "Anybody wants me I'll be in that back room." And he went off down the hall.

Not until we heard the door shut did anyone move. Outside, unseen, the hoofs of a horse made solid but diminishing lumps of sound against the empty growl of Brace's cursing.

Lupita stepped sober-faced out of the kitchen, hauling up by Oakes' chair. "You better tell him," she said.

Behind the deep crevices of shrunken cheeks Oakes sat like a mummy.

Impatience came into Lupita's black stare. "You can't hold them off without help!" A wildness got into her tones, "You better do what you have to while you've still got the —"

"Keep your voice down, you fool!"

He looked alive enough now. No matter what they were or had been to each other, it was plain her worries wasn't bothering him none. You couldn't see that look he give her and stay very solid with any other notion.

He got out of his chair and stood uncertainly silent, obviously trying to pin down what I thought. Now he nervously pawed at his scraggle of whiskers. "Reckon you kin see I'm in a pretty tight bind."

"You've sure put me into one."

Oakes, scowling fiercely, took a turn about the room. I couldn't tell, when he stopped, if it was me he was eyeing or something in his head. "How much," he said, "would it cost to put your gun on my side of this deal?"

"What's it worth?"

I could see he was worried, but even with the fright working on him he was minded to drive as stiff a bargain as he could. "Let's hear your best dollar price."

Telling him where he could go wouldn't help none. I didn't think they had swallowed that 'pardner' stuff, but I was here. And I wasn't fool enough to think they'd let me clear out.

Not, anyways, if they could help it.

I had some sharp thoughts on that subject too, but there was a heap more to this than a bunch of stole horses. "Either there's something around here them jaspers is after or they figure you're onto something they aim to be let in on."

I could see greed struggling with the fear in Oakes' look, but it was the girl that tipped his hand. She said with the words tumbling over each other, "It's the Curly Bill plunder — two wagonloads of it! All them saints he rode off with. A cigarbox of diamonds he got out of the vaults of that bank in Monterey. Thirty-nine bars —"

"You bitch!" Oakes said.

"Look at him!" she cried. "You don't have to take my word for it — *look at him!*"

The rims of Oakes' lips was the color of dust. A horrible hate was pouring out of his stare. He was so red in the face, so swelled up with rage, it was hard to put anything past him right then. Yet his voice, when he spoke, was flat as a mill pond. "You heard her," he said. "I'll split it right down the middle."

IX

He must of took me for being still wet behind the ears.

Buried treasures and maps was all over this country, likewise fools to go with them; but this Curly Bill plunder, if there was any truth to it, explained a heap that had been gnawing me. The big thing, however, that come over me right then was that Oakes wasn't figuring to split this with anyone.

You couldn't take in the scowl, and the cocked ugly shape of him, and come up with anything different. He had the look and the sound of a Simon-pure believer; and his wife was in it clean up to her lying mouth. I seen the bob of her head and her eyes, big and earnest. "A man couldn't ask for on fairer than that." She said it like Moses coming down off the mountain.

I was minded to laugh in their faces — I was riled enough to.

She put her oar in again. "With a stake like that a man could do just about anything he wanted — he could get plumb out of the scrabblin' country." When the mood was on her she could make things shine. "In Nicaragua or Chile you could both be kings."

I guess she figured this to clinch it. But alls I had to bet with was my life, and with the five of them against me I didn't need no peace twig to see it mightn't last no longer than a June frost in Tucson. I said, "How much'll half add up to?"

I guess they pegged me chump enough for anything. Oakes put another hold on his breath. "Countin' the images," he said, "an' that altar stuff, the whole thing'll figure to run at right aroun' three million."

Maybe I didn't look properly impressed.

His cheeks got dark and puffed up again. He did have the wit to keep his voice down, but you could tell by the way the words tumbled out he wasn't scarcely two jumps from going off his rocker. "It's there, every goddam bit of it! That Christ an' the Virgin is both solid gold! Forty sacks of coins, gold an' silver mixed — took a four-horse team just to haul. . . ." His eyes turned black and then jumped to mine sly like. "A cigar box crammed with diamonds! Ninety thousand Mex dollars in rawhide aparejos, thirty-nine bars of gold bullion."

"You sound powerful sure."

He clamped his choppers and stared like a bull snake. It come over me then I wasn't going at this right. "All right," I said, "but the trick is to find it. Let's see your map."

Lupita cried fiercely, "He don't need no map!

He was there with Zwing Hung when they buried it!"

Oakes, snarling, nervously peered toward the hail. "You want that sonofabitch back in here?"

A shine of sweat lay across his flesh. His eyes was like hot iron banging into her but she held her ground, giving him back look for look.

I said, "If you know where it's at why ain't you dug it up?"

"Because he's scairt," Lupita sneered, "Earp never killed Curly Bill."

"Never killed him . . ." I looked at him and then her again.

"He thinks Bill's still alive!"

"Is he?" I said, and Oakes, his stare hating her, testily growled, "You ever hear of 'em findin' his body?"

"But they shot it out —"

"You know that, do you?" Oakes pinned his glittering eyes on me. "I put in three months pawin' through that brush. *I* never found him."

We stared across a clatterous quiet.

If Earp hadn't killed him where had Brocius gone?

I'd been trying to drop out of sight myself. I hadn't left no plunder, real or imagined. I wasn't a quarter so well known as he'd been. "Well, if Wyatt didn't kill him," I finally said, "and there *was* any loot, he's probably dug it up himself."

"Sure," Oakes snorted. "Dug it up bare-handed an' packed it off in his pockets!" He peered at me contentiously. "You in this or ain't you?"

"He ain't," Ivory said from the shadows of the porch.

The surprise of it held Oakes rooted in his tracks. Lupita's blanched cheeks showed the depths of her fright, a spread of worry, the mounting flush of a furious anger. "How'd you get out there!"

Ivory chuckled. "Get rid of this feller if you want to stay healthy, Fred."

Quiet closed round us, black and deep. Chunk on chunk it rose and grew till a man scarce could breathe from the thickening of it. The feel of his eyes put the cold shivers to me. "Get rid of him tonight or he'll be got rid of for you."

X

"You talk brave as hell standing out in that dark!"

That was me, and nothing come back. You couldn't tell if he was gone or still out there.

I started for the door. Lupita, grabbing me, dug in her heels. "You want to get yourself killed!"

"If that was the answer I'd be dead right now."

Oakes, scowling, nodded. He smeared the sweat across his cheeks. His wife, turning loose of me, ran over and slammed the porch door. She put her back to it, glaring. "No tellin' what he'll do if you keep pushing at him!"

Mad and scared, her bosom heaving, she made a picture no feller with a eye for a woman could scarcely overlook.

Oakes, sunk back in his chair, was staring nastily. Then, his look finding me, he said, blowing his breath out, "Mebbe you better roll your cotton." He dug a handful of crumpled bills from his jeans and, never moving his look, flung them onto the table. "This'll take care of any time you got comin'."

I didn't say whether it would or it wouldn't.

Down the hall I threw open the first door I come to, went in, shoved it shut, and stood in dark that was blacker than stove shine. When I could make out the blobs of bed and bureau I seen a heap more I should of thought about sooner. Sometimes you wonder how crazy can you get! It wasn't the greenbacks I'd left on that table but the chance I'd passed up to climb out of this jackpot.

The goddam room didn't even have a window! And no way of keeping the door like it was without a man put the bureau to it. I wasn't about to let them hear me doing that.

A man's pride. But pride was all I'd got to show for the reckless years I'd put into a saddle. Sure, I had talents — good hand with horses, fast with a pistol. But all that last ever fetched a man is bullets.

I slumped down on the bed and took a look at myself. The things I seen didn't noways come up to the view I'd had of me. When you scraped away all the goddam twaddle I was as wild to get hold of that plunder as anyone.

I finally got around to hauling off my boots, dropped them one after the other with a jingle and thump. I sat a fidgety spell, hearing house sounds and crickets, the banged-down clatter of a sash — Ivory, likely, back inside. Come the yammering of a coyote and, presently, Oakes and Lupita shuffling past in the hall. A door opened and shut, and not even this hid away their caustic bickering.

I scowled and glared and thought some more about Ivory. Three million bucks takes a heap of getting used to. If it boiled down to no more than half that much there would still be plenty . . . for one guy, anyhow. Course there was bound to be some dying, maybe a powdersmoke payoff with myself odds-on choice for prime target.

I pushed this aside, hooked like the rest with clamorous notions of what I could do with even a piece of that plunder. It's easy to scorn greed in others, but I wasn't one to do the scorning. I wasn't counting on nothing, but it couldn't hurt to wonder what a man could do if it come to him. I sure wasn't figuring to catch me no sleep, not after what Ivory had said right in front of me.

Pure bullypuss bluff. He'd of bit and not barked if he'd been aiming to be rid of me. Still, I lifted my gun from leather before stretching out to wait for daylight.

Half a hundred things must of wheeled through my head as I laid there twisting, unable to get comfortable. Combinations I would have to watch out for as this bunch wheeled and dealed to get leverage. Wasn't a one you could trust to pass up the lion's share if he could hit on some way to get at it without being like to turn up his toes.

I clean forgot Dimity Hale in this thinking, but not Lupita, never her husband — if that's what Fred was. These were what a man had to work on, Oakes' fright and hate and Lupita's stupidity, the man hunger in her and whatever else kept pushing her into the path of Oakes' fury. These things could be used and Bill Ivory would use them. He was the one I would have to watch out for. I remembered his eyes, the cold savvy they showed, the grin that never got out of his mouth. Here was the dangerous one, not them other two.

Brace and that kid was just a couple of twisters, bad enough maybe backed into a corner but nothing to worry a man who'd been around. Stamp a boot and Brace would scuttle for cover. Alamagordo might be more stubborn, but stubborn was a horse I knowed how to handle.

Those broncs had taken out of me more than I'd reckoned. I'd of swore I never closed my eyes, but it seems I did because the next thing there was somebody out in that hall, setting each foot down quiet as a mouse.

I could feel it. Something about stealth gets into your bones.

He must have took off his boots; there wasn't a sound. I had to make myself breathe. Probably had his ear to the door, standing there listening, trying to make out if I was asleep. I done my best to convince him.

I waited and sweated, and then I knew of a sudden he was no longer out there.

I come off the bed still holding my pistol and stepped catfooted to the door in my sockfeet, listening again and then easing it open. It wasn't so black out there as inside but the hall was filled with a curdle of shadows and a current of air coldly lapped round my ankles, a warning that someone had opened the porch door.

I went forward, moving careful. I still hadn't got to the end of the hall when a board skreaked horrible under my foot. I waited till the jumpety sound of my heart quit banging my ribs, then slipped into the room where the table and chairs was.

It was dark, too, and considerable colder but not so blamed black I couldn't spot that open door. Whoever I was after must have gone outside, or was this only what they aimed for me to think? A come-on, maybe?

I stretched my ears while my eyes probed the shadows. I moved to the doorway, searching the yard with no better success, the rocks and the dark blocking me off from too much of it. Then I picked up some sound, a murmur of voices that seemed to be coming from the direction of the corrals. I supposed I ought to step out there but stood suspicious, irritably uncertain whether to go or stay put.

I didn't want to come up with any cats that curiosity had killed. That business outside my room, the open door, them voices, could all be intended to pull me out where some gent with a gun could snuff my light. At the same time I was impatiently conscious it might be some deal I wasn't to know about.

The only thing I was sure of was that, if I

stayed put, I might learn which of the ones in this house had gone out there. Actually I wasn't even sure of that; there was nothing to stop them getting in through a window. If it was Ivory out there — and he was sure as hell my favorite — he was apt as not to come swaggering cool as you please right on past me.

And there was still the back door. A man could look mighty foolish crouching over this mousehold while the sport he was hunting come in at the back.

I was minded to burn the bridge and go out there when a flutter of motion — something more sensed than seen — yanked my stare to the start of that trek through the rocks. The talking had quit and the shadows was piled so thick over there all those broncs I'd been stompin could have taken cover in them. If the goddam moon would of only come out. . . .

I sucked in my breath. Already the night was turning gray along the rim. In another couple hours the sun was due to show unless the sky was overcast, and I reckoned it was by the smell of that wind. All we needed in this deal now was a drizzling rain to make everything ducky.

Looking back at them rocks I let out a soft grunt. There was something coming out of that forest of shadows, a two-legged something, and coming straight on.

I got away from the door. Gun in hand, I backed against the wall where the murk was thickest, figuring when he come through the door to be able to gauge his size and put a name to him.

I heard bare feet cross the planks of the porch. A deeper black got into the opening, then the door was pulled shut and I still didn't know. I lashed out with the gun, felt it strike, heard a gasp and the lurching thumps of somebody staggering. Something clattered on the floor. I reached out blindly, wildly grabbing, got a fistful of cloth and felt it burn through my fingers, tearing. Then he was loose of me, gone down the hall, the sound of him lost in the rush of my breathing. I didn't even hear the goddam door shut.

I stood balked in front of the room Ivory'd taken from Brace and that feisty kid. All I could hear was the roaring pound of the blood slogging through me. It made me furious to come so close and end up with nothing.

We had made enough noise to wake John Brown, but nobody showed. I was halfway back to find out what had clattered when I realized I still had that cloth in my fist. I mighty near flung it down in disgust. It was only a scrap, and to prove anything it would have to be matched with the shirt it come off of. I couldn't see much chance of him letting that happen. I shoved it into my pocket, put the gun away, too.

I stood thinking a while, both ears cocked for trouble, then went on, thumbed a match and seen the glint winking back at me — the glint of a five-inch blade with bone handle. That's what he'd dropped, and it was sharp as a razor.

Snuffing the match I stooped, got the knife, and went back to my room with it, closing the door mighty careful behind me. It was the kind of dagger that fit into a case, perfectly balanced, somewhat short for close work but just right for throwing. I wondered how many more was around and when he would try to put one of them into me. I pushed the frog-sticker under the bureau, dug out the cloth and scratched another light.

XI

Other things can make a man stupid besides pride.

Don't ask how long I stood there. When the match got to cooking my fingers I dropped it, still seeing that twist of cloth I had hold of even after I couldn't see my own hand.

It hadn't come off no shirt I'd laid eyes to. Looked like calico ripped from a dress — a hard thing to think when you set it beside that blade I'd picked up and the time and the place and that gabble of voices. Who had she come from with a knife in her fist? and where was he now?

I was minded to look at that blade again, but even as I hitched up myself to go after it the remembered grin of that damned Bill Ivory took my thoughts down another track. Nor all her wiles couldn't turn me away from the picture of her out there with him darkly cuddled in them rocks. She was capable of it. On the porch tonight almost under Oakes' nose hadn't she squeezed my arm and give me the eye? She had no more morals than a goddam rabbit!

How else had that bunch come onto this place if somebody hadn't passed along the word? Oakes sure as hell never sent out no invites! Young as she was, time was getting away from her. Maybe she was tired of waiting on Fred. Maybe she reckoned he never would dig it up without somebody prodded him.

Still, a guy like Bill Ivory . . . I couldn't see no woman wrapping *him* around her finger. If she had started this rolling it was Brace she'd probably sent for. Then she'd happened onto me, probably scairt when he'd fetched in that kid with him; it was after they'd come she'd started giving me the business.

Ivory had been here before. Oakes had said, "You know my wife," and Ivory had asked, "Where-at's that filly you been fetchin' up for Fred?" Brace had been here, too, and he had asked about the girl, gone off hunting her. . . . Oakes telling me later he had hoped she would put a blue whistler through him.

Feller as tricky as that could have slipped outside after his wife was asleep, or after he figured she was. Him and Ivory probably caused some noise . . . that bunch of stole broncs maybe. He hadn't come before about no legend of plunder; he wasn't the kind to have left without getting his hooks on it. This had to be something new with him. It struck me he may have been watching Cort Brace. Hell! He said he'd figured Brace would probably put in here for water!

It didn't make no never-mind. A jasper like

Ivory could just about smell loot. Come to that the whole push could. I'd smelt something myself I remembered uncomfortably.

But she wouldn't kill Fred. He was the goose who knew where the eggs was — hadn't she said to me, and in considerable of a lather: *You got to keep those fools from killing Jake!* Just because she'd dropped that knife on the floor didn't prove she'd just come back from using it. Probably slipped out to gab a spell with Brace . . . that knife likely hadn't been in her hand till I jumped her.

I didn't think in them shadows she could have known it was me. She might even have thought Bill Ivory'd got hold of her. The more I woolled it around the more tangled it got me. The smart thing, I figured, was to go out and have a look. It was pretty damn sure I wouldn't catch no more shut-eye.

I shoved the rag in my pocket, shucked the spurs off my boots and, carrying them — the boots I mean, eased open the door. It was still plenty dark and quiet right now as the bottom of a pond. By considerable effort I missed the creaking board. In the sitting room I stopped for another look and listen.

If there was anything to see I certain sure missed it. Crossing the planks of the porch, balancing myself with a hand against the steps, I got into my boots.

A thin sliver of moon only made the dark chunks blacker. Half Lew Wallace's army could of been hid out in them shadows. That bed I'd give up begun to look pretty good. So would three million I reminded myself — even a chunk of it, but the thought didn't help my breathing none. It didn't help me neither to suspicion that Ivory was out there somewhere waiting with his grin for a good clean shot.

Except for the solid black of the cliffs, things at a distance you couldn't pick out at all. Even where the gloom seemed piled chunk on chunk, there wasn't enough to it to hide a man proper at scarcely less than ten paces — a sight too damned close to have to fight it out with belt guns.

I don't know why I kept picturing Ivory; it was a heap more likely she'd been out to see Brace or, just maybe, that kid. And even if it was Bill Ivory she'd been with I had no reason for supposing he'd be there now. There was something about that cold-eyed potato that kept jumping around through the tramp of my thoughts like I'd seen him before — and that didn't make much sense when you looked at it. A jasper like him a feller didn't forget.

I thought she'd come from the direction of the corrals, from the rocks anyway that hid them. It would of been some assurance to have come onto her tracks but I wasn't about to strike any matches. I was in the rocks now, trying to creep my way through and still, if I could, keep from adding my bones to the ones Oakes had showed me. I was in a fine lather, I can tell you. Only reason I didn't have hold of my pistol was I reckoned it would show up like a tin roof.

The further I went the harder it got to put one foot down ahead of the other. It's a wonder I didn't turn back. I wanted to. It made a mort of sense, but I had to see, if I was able, what she'd run with a knife from.

She wouldn't of been much beyond them next rocks because the pens, I figured, was right there behind them; and, probably, Brace and the kid. And maybe Bill Ivory just waiting for me.

I would sooner of took a beating than step around them rocks, but I knew I had to do it. The dark slid up around my chest and lapped around my neck like water, cold and black as a cartload of stove lids, and the quiet got thick enough to chop with an ax. He was there, and he was waiting, though I didn't straight-off see him.

What my stare latched onto was this crumpled-up blotch all spraddled out like a bunch of dropped clothes. A stiff, of course. You don't have to get down and rassle them around to know when a guy ain't got no pressing use for boot jacks.

I was right about him waiting but wrong about the pens. It was the next rocks they was back of. It was when I looked to find them I seen Ivory's teeth grinning out of the shadows. He said, powerful soft, "Scratch a match an' roll him over."

He must of thought I couldn't tell skunks from house cats. I said, "You want him over, turn him."

There was a heap of ugliness breathed into the silence while I fished out my pipe and thumbed fresh smoking. It done me good to feel his temper and know Flick Farsom, by grab, had outfoxed him. If he'd been going to shoot he'd have shot in the first place.

It was this, and him holding his voice down, that woke me up to who had the choice. For some reason he wanted to keep this just between him and me. I should of looked that part of it over more careful.

I seen him folding his arms. He said, "You know who this is?"

"Don't look like Fred Oakes. Bony enough, maybe, but —"

"Ain't Brace, neither. You reckon it's that kid?"

I took another squint. Then it come over me what he was getting at.

Ivory nodded. "Looks like somebody else has bought into this. You got any notion how he got here, or when?"

I shook my head.

"You reckon he just sort of stumbled into it?"

Both the place and the time was against it. "Maybe," I said, "we better look for his horse."

"What I want to know," Ivory said, "is who got him here."

I could feel the black drill of his gaze boring into me. All the good feeling had turned to bile in my throat. From here on out he would be watching his chance to get rid of me.

For all I knew he may have got rid of this guy.

I said, "Could be he just happened by and dropped in, some old friend of Fred's."

Even to me it didn't sound likely.

"There wasn't no horse sound," Ivory said. "I got here just as whoever dropped him cleared out. Wasn't no sound at all."

"Then how —"

"The breath was still whistling out of him."

It put a cold shiver through me. Watching him that way, seeing him plainer, it come to me that daylight wasn't far off. "If they knocked him down with a gun barrel. . . ."

Ivory said, "It wasn't no gun barrel."

"But if there'd been a shot . . ." I stopped, silent, staring, as Brace and the kid stepped around the boulders that blocked us off from any sight of the corrals. I thought Alamagordo was going to walk right into the corpse before he seen it. Brace, a little ahead of him, turned handily aside but the kid, when he spotted it, stopped so short he had to throw out both arms for balance. Ivory, watching, kept his notions to himself. The kid said, "Jesus!" and his eyes looked round as marbles.

Brace was trying too hard. It just wasn't natural he should be so near and never once bat his glance in that direction. "What's the row?" he growled testily. "You goin' to wrangle like cats on a back fence all night?"

He knew better than the kid did what was there. But they hadn't been listening, or been together long, else Alamagordo would of played the same tune.

Brace done his best. As though just waking up he kind of stiffened in his tracks, let the jump of his stare be drawn behind him and down. Ivory, not waiting for any more, said, "Turn him over, and let's have a look at him."

The light was bettering fast. The tinhorn looked like something hacked out of cardboard.

"Go on — he won't bite," Ivory said. "Hurry up, I'm gettin' hungry."

You'd have thought, the way he stood, Brace couldn't bring himself to bend. But he done it, turned him; then shot up to twist away, puking, and I didn't much blame him.

There was a gaping slash beneath the stiff's chin, dark with blood, where his throat had been cut. It was the kid's skreaky voice that put the name to him. "Billy Grounds!" he gasped, and his face was wet with the sweat of terror.

The hair on the back of my own neck stirred. Billy Grounds had been killed several years ago during a fight at the Stockton ranch.

XII

Must be some mistake, I thought, scowling at the shaking shape of Cort Brace, wondering how much he knew about this, wondering which and how many of us would be picking up cards from this deal tomorrow. Cold and sharply sliding through a churned-up welter of floundering confusions was the feel of my arm squeezed against her bosom, the clatter of that blade and the gravelly sound of her wildly shouting, "You got to keep those fools from killing Jake!"

I couldn't help thinking this was one way to do it.

Ivory said to Brace in the same kind of tone he might of spoke about the weather, "You still packing that pig sticker you used to pare your nails with?"

The gambler jerked up his head in a disbelieving stare. He might not have been no picture of innocence, but shifty or not he looked plenty affronted. "You think I could do a thing like that!"

"Somebody done it." A cruel amusement crinkled Ivory's mouth. "For three million smackers any one of us could — and I ain't countin' out Jake or that double-breasted whore. Now get out of those boots."

I noticed the cold in the widening quiet that abruptly appeared to be everywhere about us. In this gray light it must of seemed like to Brace, with them hard eyes cracking into him, he didn't have the chance of a snowball in hell.

Shivering, whimpering, the rabbity face of him twitching and jerking, he got down on his butt.

"The other one, Sweetheart. The one with the knife in it."

Visibly wilting, Brace switched his hold.

"I don't think he done it."

Above the black mustache Ivory's look reached across in a hard, searching scrutiny. "Someone asked for your notion?"

I don't know why I should of took up for Brace except it was the remembrance of what was under my bureau. The tinhorn had known, before he'd come butting in, what they was going to run into. Look at the way he'd stepped around that stiff!

Now he'd got off his boot. The hilt of a knife stuck out from it plain. "Still reckon he didn't do it?"

Without the patronizing mockery oozing up out of the sneer of that question I might have turned loose of Brace, remembering the girl. But Ivory's assumption of always having the answers to everything gravelled me. "It don't have to follow, because he's got a knife, Brace used it to cut that whipporwill's throat."

"You got a better prospect?"

The smugness of it woke me like a hoof in the gut. I'd been took like a kid, led by the nose and — oh, sweet Jesus!

Bully Brace was just a dodge Ivory'd used, a strawman set up to coax past locked faces any knowledge of suspicions we might think to hide away from him. To me it was the measure of an inexcusable carelessness — my own, because I'd marked Bill Ivory the first time I'd seen him as a lobo among the foxes, a real plumb cultus hombre, a Ketchum romping with a bunch of fool Sam Basses.

He seen how I felt, enjoyed every bit of it. The sly goad of his chuckle nearly pushed me past the last grab of caution, so goddam mad I could cheerfully of belted him. One thing it done — nothing could of dragged me out of this now. I meant to beat that son of a bitch if it killed me.

Fred Oakes come round from the house, snatched one look at that face-up stiff and cringed like he had took a mortal hurt. He went a fish-belly white, staggered back a couple paces with his jaw dropped down like a hoofshaper's apron. He pulled a shuddering breath and tried to scrape himself together.

"How about it, Jake?" Ivory said smooth as silk. "Cort allows you've run with most of the bad boys. You got a handle for this feller?"

Oakes' mouth worked but nothing came out of

it. On the ground Brace reached for the boot he'd took off. Ivory said, "You're not goin' anywhere," and hooked the boot with a foot clean out of Brace's reach. "Well, Jake, speak up," he grinned. "You ever seen him before?"

It was cold in them rocks but the glint of sweat could be seen in Fred's whiskers. He wiped the hands against his pants. "Billy Grounds," he wheezed, shuddering.

Ivory considered him. "Didn't I hear Grounds was killed in that ranch fight at Stockton's?"

"The dead walk in these hills," Fred groaned. He grabbed a fresh breath with the hate twisting through him so naked you could hear it. "You might try kickin' him up like you done that greaser down to Uvalde. Go on — kick him. Couldn't be you're scairt of a dead hant, could it? The great king —"

Ivory caught the old coot such a clout in the face I half looked for his fist to come out the other side. It didn't, of course — didn't make much improvement to Fred's looks, neither. Blood spurted from his nose, brightening up his whiskers as he went reeling back to come down hard on his butt in a jounce of loosed air.

I looked for the old fool to break right out and bawl. He brought a hand from the dirt, whimpering like a cur no more than it touched the pulpy wreck of his beak. Staring at the blood he hauled himself to his feet. "All I said —"

"I heard what you said," Ivory told him, spider soft. "Now get on up to the house — and set out some grub before, by God, I really work you over."

The grub was all fried up and waiting, which was probably what Oakes had come out to tell us — flapjacks and sowbelly and a great heaping platter of warmed-over frijoles. Fred's wife had done herself proud, she truly had. But anyone who looked to find a welcome mat out was going to have to put on his fine-print cheaters.

Oakes didn't come tramping in with the rest but cut off around to the side where the spring was. Since he might have a pistol, though he'd left off his shell belt, I rather expected Ivory to order him back. He never even looked to see where Fred was headed for.

After we set down and everyone had dug in or was fixing his grub to suit, Ivory said, "Eating, with me, is a solemn occasion. When I put on the feed bag I don't take kindly to people junin' around."

She give him a bitter look but set. It didn't have no effect on her tongue, though. "Where's Fred?" she demanded.

"Can't you stand for him to be out of your sight for ten minutes?"

Before she could fly back Fred came in. He hauled up his chair. His nose looked powerful painful, but he'd scrubbed all the gore out of his scraggle of whiskers. He pitched in without speaking after Lupita, still riled, had filled his plate. It was plain she was busting to sound off some more but with Ivory leaning into his food like he was I guess she figured it was best not to bother him.

Maybe you're thinking it was strange, after the deal Oakes had offered — half of everything split straight down the middle, I hadn't taken up for him when Ivory hung that fist in his face. First place, Fred looked the kind that in a bind would offer a man the moon if he had to. Bets made on the strength of any deal with him would be plum off, I figured, the minute he got out from under.

I suppose I might of put in my oar if Ivory, instead of popping him, had made a stab for his pistol. As things turned out I was plenty content to rock along with the rest. I'd be having my turn with him soon enough without bringing anything on premachoorly. I wasn't — even to myself — ready yet to admit there could be any doubts which of us would bait coyotes when the smoke rolled away.

There wasn't much question about Ivory's caliber — it ain't barking dogs you got to watch out for. Back of his grins he was rough as a cob. Touch iron around him and you'd be like to have to use it.

Oakes didn't appear to be overly hungry. The girl, too, only kind of picked at her food. The kid ate strong, his spare time being divided pretty even between surly glances first at Ivory, then at me. Brace's hands shook so bad he finally give it up. When we'd left that corpse Bill had fetched along Brace's boot — had it setting right up on the table beside him. When he swabbed out his plate and set back, I done likewise.

He was a cool one, all right. He could beat around the bushes or come straight at a thing blunt enough to make a stone twitch. Now, passing out the smiles, he said, "We didn't none of us ride out here to hunt mosquitoes. Before we bring this meeting to order you got any thoughts, Jake, you'd admire to unload?"

Fred's eyes flapped around like two flies in a bottle. "I don't guess," he got out, "you'd be settin' no store by my gab if I had."

"You got every right to speak if you want," Ivory said, teeth shining. "In a deal like this its best to all be equal partners, poolin' everything we know. That way we can be sure no one's cheatin'. It's share and share alike or we come right up against them plain hard facts we seen out there in the rocks. Reckon none of us is anxious to feed the buzzards. Long's we act like gents there won't nobody have to, if you get what I mean.

"Now, we've got this boot," he said, picking it up, "and we'ye got that stiff." He slid the knife up and down a few times in the leather. "Boot belongs to Cort, we all seen him get out of it; so it's reasonable to figure this Arkinsaw toothpick's his too. I'm not sayin' he killed that feller. If the jigger's Billy Grounds . . . hell! Mebbe the guy ain't Grounds at all. The dead may walk in these hills like Jake says, but I would personal want a little more than his word for it. Thing I'm tryin' to bring out is, if we don't want corpses stacked up all around we better make out to be a mite more co-operative."

Brace, by the scowl of him, had picked up the message. Oakes settled deeper into his chair, but all it got out of the kid was a sneer. He sure picked the times to expose his ignorance.

What I wanted myself was another look at that blade — not the one in Brace's boot but the knife someone lost in the dark of the hall when I'd struck out with my gun. I knew it hadn't been Oakes'. I wasn't sure it was his wife, but that cloth I'd yanked loose hadn't come off no shirt.

So unless it was Lupita, it must of been Dimity Hale. She could easy have ridden in, I thought. What was harder to figure was what she'd been up to before she had fetched the corpse. It could explain how he'd come into this deal. It didn't account for everything though — his condition, for one. Had he arrived as dead freight? Quick or dead he must of come on a horse — and what about the muddle of voices I'd heard just ahead of whoever had slipped into the house?

Every trail a man took brought him back to that knife — and it might, even in daylight, be clean as a new pin. First chance I got I meant to look.

There was a heap in this deal I couldn't latch onto. I was riled and excited and crammed with frustrations, but of one thing I was pretty well convinced. If Oakes was Jake Gauze, and this dead guy was Grounds, there was sure as hell some kind of plunder to be had — and it wasn't far off.

XIII

“Well,” Ivory said, “What’s it going to be — dog eat dog, or a little sweetness and light?”

He flashed his tough grin, settling back, crossing his arms. Didn’t seem much doubt what the upshot would be. Greed and envy and fear was coming out of Brace like water from a rusty tub. Hate shone like a lantern in Lupita’s bitter stare, and Fred Oakes didn’t look much happier than a weasel with his backend caught in a bear trap.

Only the kid looked to have any spunk and, as usual, he picked the wrong time to parade it. He said with his lip pulled into a snarl, “You think we’re dumb enough to swaller that?”

A cheap crook like Brace would have swarmed all over him. Ivory laughed it off. Big and easy, he said, “Believe what you like but give it a try. There’s plenty in this for all of us. I know you’re thinkin’ I been fixing to grab the lion’s share. Well, I just plain can’t, and you can’t neither. Nobody here by himself is goin’ to do it.”

He slanched the brash glint of his shrewd stare

around. "We got to be practical. With all of us pulling together, and everybody watching everybody else, there's a pretty fair chance we can all come out well-heeled. I leave it up to you."

He had a real talking talent. I suspect there was other things up his sleeves that he would probably trot out when it suited him. He slipped the knife from Cort's boot and run his thumb along the edge in such a offhand show you couldn't help thinking. I seen Brace shiver.

Fred's wife squeezed her eyes shut. When they flew open she said, "I'm for poolin'."

"Figures," Oakes sniffed. "I notice them that's got the least is generally agreeable to addin' to it. How do you vote, Farsom?"

"Reckon I'll have to string along with the lady."

His stare raked Brace and the kid and come away. I suppose he found the situation intolerable; he showed his contempt. "All right." He glared at Ivory. "Where you figure to go from here?"

Bill, putting the knife back, hauled the lips off his teeth. "Why, Jake, old horse, we're leavin' that up to you."

The only think Oakes' face give away was his temper.

Ivory, watching, lazily smiling, said, "You're the nearest thing to Curly Bill a man's like to get his hands on now."

"Let me work him over," Brace said. Nobody paid any attention to Brace.

"If there's anything buried and Fred knows where it's at," I put in, "why ain't he dug it up and took off?"

"Yeah," Alamagordo said, "how come?"

Ivory chuckled. "What would the rest of you do in Jake's boots if you had it in your heads Curly Bill might be lurkin' just around the next rock?"

Brace showed the whites of his eyes. "That's crazy!" the kid cried. "Wyatt Earp emptied a shotgun into Bill at Iron Springs . . ."

Oakes showed the snags of his yellowed teeth. "You help bury him? You was there, I presume?"

That meanness come into the kid's look again. "Plenty others was there!"

"Well," Fred said, "you think what you want an' I'll do the same." He scrubbed a hand through his whiskers, took his look back to Ivory. "The unvarnished truth of the matter is I wasn't around when that plunder got buried. I don't know no more about it than you do."

Lupita, whirling in a rustle of skirts, grabbed onto Bill Ivory. "He ain't spent all this time around here just to keep hid out from any bunch of damned stranglers!"

"Say! That's right," the kid grinned, "Jake Gauze was s'posed to been strung up, wasn't he? Somethin' about a horse . . ."

"And Grounds, that's out in those rocks with his throat slit, was supposed to been killed in that Stockton ranch fight," Ivory purred. "And Zwing Hunt, you'll remember, is said to have been buried at the mouth of this canyon in a scrub oak's shake. Accordin' to his uncle over at San Antone, that ain't so at all. By his tell Hunt come clean back to Texas where he died a few weeks later after gulpin' out this yarn of buried plunder."

"It ain't no yarn," Lupita said waspishly, "it's the God's own truth! He even made a map! Jake's got . . ." Stopping, startled, she clapped a hand to her mouth.

"Now," Ivory smiled, "we're getting somewheres. Not that I put any great stock in maps. If it comes to that I got a couple myself. But with Jake bein' close as he was to Curly Bill —"

"Grounds was closer," Oakes said, getting up. "Bill never buried it. He give that chore to Grounds an' Hunt, which is why Zwing let out fer Texas like he done. All Bill knowed about where the stuff was is what they told him. He was powerful anxious to come up with those boys. Facts is, he was huntin' them when he ran into Earp at Iron Springs."

"And it's your contention Earp never killed him?"

"Think what you want," Oakes said, glaring. "The Tombstone *Nugget* offered ten hundred dollars fer a look at the body. Nobody ever walked off with that dinero. Nobody ever turned up Bill's bones. If he's dead where's his carcass?"

The kid, I seen, was staring hard at Bill Ivory. Brace, too, was looking uneasily nervous. Had I missed my bets? Was Ivory really Brocius? Even allowing for the changes time might have wrought I still didn't think so. To my mind Ivory wasn't right for the part. In lots of ways he was I reckoned, but Oakes would know. If this feller was really Curly Bill, Oakes was a heap better actor than I was ready to admit; and I found myself considering Lupita. If Ivory wasn't Brocius, who in the devil's name was he! While he may not have fit my ideas of Curly Bill, he fit a heap less the role of shoot-and-fly gunslick. Too shrewd he looked, too smooth and deadly.

Oakes said abruptly, "If that stiff is Grounds, whoever made meat of him either didn't know him or never looked beyond his nose. Because why? Because, aside from Zwing Hunt — that we can take it fer gospel is sure enough dead, he was the only jasper still afoot that knowed where the plunder was planted."

Consternation climbed into the look of Cort Brace. Lupita turned livid. Alamagordo, the kid, begun throatily to curse, opening and closing his fists in balked fury while he glowered first at Ivory, then, wickedly, at me. It was plain he figured, in what he used for a mind that one or the other of us had done Grounds in. Yet it was him that had put the name to Grounds first and Oakes that had confirmed it.

Ivory, apparently plowing the same furrow, took hold of Fred with a narrowing glance. "You said the guy *was* Grounds. Now you say *if* he was Grounds. You can't have it both ways. Is he or ain't he?"

Oakes pawed his whiskers. "I thought first off he was. But —"

"Now you ain't so sure. That what you're trying to say?"

Fred looked confused. Ivory said, "You better look again then. Come on. You, too, Farsom."

I didn't know Billy Grounds from Adam's off ox but it didn't seem to be the right time to argue it. I followed Fred out, Ivory trailing behind us, Brace and the kid wheeling through the door after him. Brace said, "How's about givin' me back that boot?"

Ivory, with the boot tucked under an arm, never turned his head. His eyes, when I looked back, was bright and watchful as a magpie's. Was it me he mistrusted or Fred? Probably, I suspected, both of us. Brace looked minded to reach for his gun, eyes wild and scairt enough for pretty near anything. It was the look of the kid that really gouged me. There was a chessycat grin pulling back his lips as he come limping after us.

I heard Ivory closing up. We was into the rocks, twisting and turning, following that snake's hips wiggle of a path, and he was sure not figuring to be treated to no surprise. Fred, I thought, you could pretty well figure. That kid was the one had me fighting my hat. I'd of give something to know what he found so damn funny.

It was getting hot fast with the sun beating down like the flat of a hammer when I rounded a twist and walked hard into Fred, grabbing onto him for balance. He grunted as the breath flew out of me. Then I seen what had stopped him and turned rigid as he was, eyes stiff with shock.

You ain't going to guess what was there, so I'll tell you. Nothing, by God, but a empty path and that dark gob of blood. The sound of stirred-up flies, and Bill Ivory back of me sucking his wind showed he seen the same things. Just the rocks and the dust and that blacked-over muck where Grounds had got his throat cut. The corpse was gone.

XIV

One thing come into my head straightaway — the face of Dimity Hale, and I sure as hell hated it. Scowling and squirming wouldn't butter no parsnips. It had to be her. No one else had the chance, we'd been all cooped up together in the house.

More I thought about it more convinced I got. She could of pulled him into this; greed wasn't just for the bastards, it could break out in anyone. And even if she hadn't — had just stumbled onto him out of the blue, it was her had took Grounds away from here.

Nothing else made sense . . . unless you could make out to believe there was more of them. I plain couldn't do it; and no more did I figure Brace and that kid, or Ivory either, had just happened to show when they had. Place was too well hid, too unhandy to get to. These rannies, I'm damn sure, were sent for.

Brace, I suspected, had been sucked in by Lupita; maybe not the same way she had got me out here, but the fact that she had was a step toward believing. Fed up with Fred, half out of her mind, she'd likely figured with his help to grab what she could and light out for new pastures. She'd have ways to get at Brace, no trouble there. She was the kind to tie more than one string to her bow, which was where I come in. But when the gambler showed up with the kid she'd got scairt — that was the way I sized it up anyway.

Grounds was something else. According to Oakes he'd been the last man alive to know for a fact where the plunder was planted. Ivory, on his own word for it, had been expecting Brace. Both of them had been here before. There was nothing at all to show Grounds had ever been here, no reason for him being here now unless it would be the Curly Bill loot.

Had Oakes sent for Grounds? Before these others had turned up he might of. Fred might know just enough to feel likely he could talk his way into a pretty fair slice of it. Only Fred and the kid appeared to know Grounds by sight. The kid hadn't killed him — not to my notion. Brace, when he'd come onto us before, had already known there was a stiff laying there, and Brace had been packing a knife. But one of Fred's women had had a knife on her too, the one I'd picked up and shoved under my bureau. And I was pretty sure now the one I'd grabbed was Lupita, but that didn't mean she had used it on Grounds. Had Fred cut his throat?

Behind me Ivory said, "Well!" and repeated it.

Nobody else seemed to have wind enough. Brace and the kid fanned out beside us. "Now that he's got up and took himself off," Ivory said in Fred's direction, you come any nearer to putting a tag to him?"

Oakes scarcely grunted, looking more than ever like something put out to keep the birds off the crops. Ivory's mouth, tightening up, shaped its cold thin grin while his eyes got narrower and darker till a gusty breath fell out of him. His voice when he spoke was considerable changed. Temper was scratching through, giving out in rumblings of impatience. "You think I been talkin' to hear my head rattle?"

He reached out then quick, uncoiling like a cougar, and the slap of his hand back and forth across Oakes' cheeks was like the flat of a board coming against a mare's behind. "By God we don't have to keep you alive!"

It brought Fred back like nothing else could have. The loony look went out of his stare. He stumbled off a couple of teetering steps, got hold of his balance and stood there unwinking.

Ivory's eyes looked as bleak as two bullets. "Now I'll ask you once more to put a name to that corpse."

"It was Grounds, right enough," Fred grumbled.

"You send for him?"

"No."

"Well, somebody did. And I'll tell you something else. He was dead as a doornail. So unless you got more of Bill's gang cached around —"

"Jesus Christ!" Oakes said, desperate, "I never even knowed he was here, damn it!"

"Then that Hale filly moved him. Where is she?"

Oakes licked his lips. "She's supposed to be out there watchin' them broncs."

"Farsom," Ivory said, "go find her." Never taking his look off Fred, he growled, "Throw some feed to whatever's in the pens and see can you turn up the nag Grounds come in on." He stood there a moment with his eyes flattening out. "While the rest of us is waiting we'll be studying Jake's map."

Oakes, scowling ugly, headed back the way we'd come, Ivory herding the other two after him. Going on to the corrals I dumped grain in a nosebag and hung it on Fred's mouse.

There was only one other horse in sight, probably Ivory's, a three-stockinged roan. I shook him down a armful of hay. Neither my dun nor any of the others the kid had run out of these pens had come back; and while I was standing there I reckoned it might come in handy was I to take along this roan. Be a really good chance for me to get plumb out. And if I pushed along the broncs I'd have the makings of a stake and I wouldn't have to risk being carved up to get it.

It was the most sensible notion I'd had since gettin' here, but of course I wasn't about to run out on three million dollars, nor anybody else. No matter how many horses was left to climb onto.

I grabbed a handful of mane, stripped off the bag and slipped my bridle onto Fred's big grulla. I got a blanket on his back, added my saddle and worked out the wrinkles before yanking the trunk strap. I thumped a knee against his belly and took up the slack. The old skate grunted like he'd rollers in his nose.

I went back and cut for sign, finding about what I'd reckoned I would. I seen where she'd hoisted him onto her horse. Lucky Grounds wasn't bigger; even so she'd had her hands full the way that horse had kept sidling around trying to get away from the blood stink.

Pretty soon I come onto heavier sign where she'd added her weight to what the horse had to carry. These tracks I followed through the dust of the gut. Wasn't no place else she could go from here but off down canyon to where I'd worked them broncs. I was too anxious to come up with her to waste any time hunting around for Grounds' horse. Settling back in the leather, half fried from the heat trapped between these walls, I let Fred's horse pick his gait through the shale and bleached bones left behind — according to Fred — by dead smugglers.

A creepy place and a hateful one. I was glad enough to have better things to ponder, like what I would do with my share of the loot if we found anything and I could get clear with it. Wasn't likely to be easy; wouldn't none of that bunch give a inch without he had to.

Brace's rabbity face come into my thoughts,

and the kid's mean look and Jake, Fred Oakes, or whatever his name was, and the scairt jiggly ways of his unstable wife. Wasn't a one of them to be trusted any further than you could throw them. But they was all of a kind compared to Bill Ivory. Fume and stew like a basket of snakes, twisting and hissing and showing their fangs.

They was beauties, all right, but Ivory was the one I looked at the longest. Fear didn't have no holds on that tiger. What he figured to do he would do if it killed him.

I kept coming back to this same notion. It was the others a man would better keep both his eyes on. Till the plunder was found I needn't worry about Ivory. I would as soon have forget about Lupita but I couldn't.

Her or Brace was to my way of thinking the most likely agents for what had happened to Grounds. I wanted another good look at that knife before I'd be satisfied which had done it; and maybe not even then, for there was always Fred Oakes. Fred had mighty sure known him.

He might of fixed it so Grounds would pop out here. It wasn't impossible. And if he'd got what he wanted — maybe more if he hadn't, he was in pretty deep. He had the pushiest reason, but Lupita and Brace was the ones with the knives. At least Brace had sure as hell had one. And he was twisty, conniving — but no more than Fred's woman. It give me a turn to remember the feel of her snuggling up to me, hugging my arm. I'd plumb forgot all about that.

Where the red sandstone walls opened out around the broncs in that waving lemon carpet of grass she was standing, watching, with the wind in her hair, with it slapping like shot through her man's hickory shirt. She made a sight I can tell you, slim as a boy except where her breasts was.

She didn't call, didn't wave, never backed off a foot, just kept standing there waiting with that Sharps in her hands, watching me come up with her sea-green stare hard and bright as jagged glass.

"Far enough!" she sung out before I got in good belt-gun range. "You got somethin' to say you can say it right there, then turn that nag and git back where you come from!"

Didn't seem like she was minded to waste much breath. In my thoughts she hadn't been so sharp, nor half as handsome as she looked right then. I said, halfway riled, "Bein's I've rode clear out here you might at least listen."

"Just come right out with it. I can hear you."

"What I come to say was for your ear alone, and if that's the best welcome you got you can keep it." Saying which with a scowl I yanked the grulla's head around and was fixing to beat on his ribs with my heels when curiosity, like I figured, got the best of her.

"Just a minute!" she called. I looked over my shoulder. "If you can't trust me," I said, "let's forget the whole business."

She'd half lowered the rifle but she could bring it into line with my name mighty quick. I reckoned she had plenty of reason to be cagey considering the sort of folks she'd be used to, rimrock riders and drifting gunslicks, Oakes and Lupita and tinhorns like Brace. You could see she was weighing remembered indignities against the risks of letting me nearer.

I said, disgusted, "I never bit you before."

"You never got no chance. That's Fred's private horse you're forkin', mister. He'll lift the roof clean off the rafters."

"There's a new, bigger dog barkin' back there now. Oakes ain't piping the tunes no more."

"What you done — shot him?"

"Ma'am, this yelling is ruinin' my throat."

Way them eyes stared back would have shook a brass monkey. My clothes felt like I'd been out in a dew. "All right," she nodded, "peel out of that shell belt. Loop it over your horn. Now git off that grulla and come up slow."

It was plain enough she wasn't no fool. What wasn't so sure was how far she'd go if something I done throwed her into a tantrum. There ain't many things more crazy to prod than a itchy-fingered female crouched back of a firearm. I say I kept this in mind every step of the way. You'd have thought Polite was my middle name.

She let me come up to within ten foot. "That'll be fine," she said. "I guess we can hear each other plain enough now."

For all that her voice sounded cool as a pig on

a platter of ice there was a prickle of sweat across the top of her lip and I could see a pulse thumping in the hollow of one cheek.

Her tone got impatient. "You goin' to stand there all day?"

"Ma'am," I said, mighty edgy, "what'd you do with him?"

"If you're speakin' of Grounds I buried him — what else?"

I don't mind telling you it give me a turn, her talking so offhand about that corpse. Made me narrow my eyes, trying to read her better. "How'd you know what his name was?"

"He ate here last night. Said his name was Grounds and he'd come huntin' Fred."

"Say what he wanted with him?" She shook her head. I said, "Come up, you mean, from the San Simon?"

"He come through the fence."

"That's all you know about him?"

Her eyes swept my face, and I could almost of swore I seen the glint of hidden laughter. "How much do you know?"

I was under a strain, of course, and confused. I growled, "Accordin' to Fred he was the last guy —" and stopped, staring furious.

"Oh, you don't have to hide it. I know all about that mule team of plunder." A small, taunting smile struck across her mouth. "Poor Fred, I guess he'll never git over it." She stepped back with her eyes, green as grass, opening wide.

"Don't tell me you been took in by it, too!"

I peered at her uneasily. The rush of horrid thoughts through my mind come unsettling and raucous as a stampede of cattle.

"You honestly believe Curly Bill's still alive?" She put back her head in a fine show of scorn. "You figure he's trampin' around through these hills still tryin' to come up with a treasure that never existed outside them crazy dreams of Zwing Hunt? A cigar box of diamonds! Forty aparejos crammed with Mexican silver! Bars of bullion! Plaster saints made of solid gold! Farsom, you astonish me — I never would of guessed you had a noggin full of pigeons."

XV

I could of took open laughter just as easy. I was sick as a man can afford to get, feeling mean all through and horrible used. I reached for my pipe, jerking away the hand in a haze of red fury so violent it shook me. I had to clench my fists to keep them from trembling. And then, needing something to hit, I snarled, "You callin' Lupita loco too?"

"She's got it bad as Fred," Dimity said.

"And how do you explain Billy Grounds showing up? One of the pair that —"

"I'm tryin' to tell you. Grounds never buried a thing in these hills."

"You're wasting your breath. Grounds wouldn't come —"

"That's just it," she insisted. "He did. He come up to show Fred the whole thing was a hoax. Him and Zwing Hunt made it up for laughs."

"Some laugh!" I said, bitter. "I don't believe it."

Color jumped into her cheeks and ran out.

Her finger curled white round the grip of that trigger. "Be a fool then! Go on and git yourself killed!"

"I don't see Brace —"

"That tinhorn!" she looked her contempt. "Cort Brace ain't got sense enough to blow out a lamp."

"You lumpin' Ivory in that, too?"

"Ivory!" Her eyes opened wide. "Has he been back?"

"He's took over this deal."

She stood post stiff for about six heartbeats. The rifle sagged in her hands. "Flick — I'm scairt."

"I'm astonished," I said, giving her back some of her own. "Ain't that somethin' of a comedown f—"

"Be still!" She chewed at her lip. There was almost a sadness to the look of her then, a kind of defeat that seemed unbearable. I had a crazy impulse to reach out and grab her, and probably I should of. Then her glance swept up. Her face cleared like magic. "Of course!" she cried. "He's come after his horses."

"If you're meaning these broncs," I said, glad of the chance, "you can forget 'em right now. He's talkin' treasure and offering shares to anyone who'll help him lay hold of it."

Half shut eyes hid away her thoughts. But she wasn't licked yet. It was in the way her chin come up, in the hard-edged way she pushed out her words. "Fred'll never do it!"

"He'll do it," I growled. "He'll either do it or die."

Her hand caught my arm. "You don't understand!"

She looked mixed up and frightened, like only just now was she coming to grips with this. She said, terrible earnest, "That treasure's Fred's life."

"Thought you claimed there wasn't no treasure?"

"In Fred's mind there is."

"You bet!" I grinned. "He sure ought to know. He was with Curly Bill when they throwed down on them smugglers, and Christ knows how many other deals, too."

Her eyes was bigger. Her fingers was like steel hooks on my arm. "Flick, you've got to help him!"

"*Got* to?" She must of seen something of what I was feeling. She let go and stepped back, her face strangely different. She started, timid, to put out her hand. "Flick . . . ?"

Whatever was eating her she pushed it aside and, though the jumpety pulse was still beating her cheek, she spoke cool enough. "You've got to make them see there isn't any plunder."

"And how do I do that?"

"Convince Ivory."

She was perfectly serious. I seen right then she didn't know Ivory. I didn't know the sonofabitch either, but I could see well enough no remarks of mine was going, even partway, to turn him around. Whoever he was, wherever he'd come from, he was here for one thing. It looked to me like he'd get it.

"Now you listen," I told her. "Thing for you to do is get clean out of this. Pronto! You and these broncs — if you don't go lallygaggin' round picking daisies, can be halfway to Christmas before that bunch ever finds out you're gone. Go on," I growled, "start roundin' 'em up while I'm pullin' this fence down."

Figuring I was being a heap more noble than the girl had any call to expect, I was hiking for the brush Fred had stacked across the trail when some half grabbed notion jerked me about for another look. Her eyes met mine. She hadn't moved a inch.

"Don't you savvy plain English?"

"Fred's been good to me."

For a moment I glared, too whipped to cuss. The idea of a shoot-and-run bastard like Jake going out of his way to be good for anyone looked about as likely as a growed bull in bloomers.

The wind shouldered into me, snapping out the manes and tails of the broncs, scooting off like shadows through the twisting folds of that flattening grass.

There was no sense trying to talk him down to her. I could still snake her out of this, taking her myself, and if we sent these nags pounding down the trail it looked a fair enough chance — with one horse between them, they would never catch up. But was that what I wanted?

I stomped back to her, scowling. I didn't want to see her hurt, wasn't anxious to think of her being around when Ivory begun to turn rough and get ugly, which he sure as hell would and mighty quick if Fred balked. But I didn't crave either to be left out if it happened she was wrong and they come up with that plunder. I didn't see how she could possibly be right. Brace I could discount same as she did, but a feller just couldn't look at Ivory and believe it. Conviction lurked in every twist of his grin.

She watched me out of a wooden face. The Sharps still hung at arm's length from one fist and the other was halfway up to her throat, dangling there like a hawk in the blue. She must of sensed . . . her woman's intuition must have told her I wasn't going along with her notions.

She didn't yell or cuss, tear into me or nothing. Her eyes, big again, got dark and glimmery. Her raised hand dropped like a gut-shot duck.

"Flick —" The word come out of her thin as a whisper. I watched her swaller. "I'm so terrible helpless." A kind of shiver ran all the way through her.

I stood there, scowling, knowing what she was up to, feeling the heat piling into my cheeks and not able for hell to get my talk going. There was a ache in my arms — I tried to snort it away. I had a chance in this deal to come out fixed for life, and only a nump would pitch it aside like a busted pot on account of a woman he didn't scarcely know even. It was Fred she was worried about, not me! Fear had got her backed into a corner. *Pity her, sure, but don't let her push you out of the boat. She's trying to help Fred. You can see that, can't you?*

It was why she had told them lies. I said, bitter, "Fred don't need you or me to speak for him. Did you send for Grounds? Was it you got him out here?"

"I never laid eyes on him before last night."

Then why was she watching so breathless and bright? "Why'd you move him?" I said, almost hating her. "How'd you know he was there to be moved?"

"I was worried." She begun twisting her hands around the snout of that Sharps. "You'd of been too, knowin' Grounds had gone up there to tell them the truth. I didn't know about Ivory, but Brace had been creepin' around here before, mumblin' at Fred and actin' like —"

"Fred! Why are you all the time calling him Fred? Don't you know he's Jake Gauze?"

Her eyes never said whether she did or she didn't.

"He was one of the bunch that jumped them smugglers. A cow thief and horse thief!" I said, warming up to it. "A murderin' killer what's spent half his life dodgin' hemp and sheriffs' posses!"

Her eyes was like glass.

"You got proof of that, have you?"

"Go ask his wife!"

She skinned back her lips. I never ketched what she said, it sounded like *pooda.* She grabbed a fresh breath. "When I got to the pens I could hear someone arguin'. Just the sounds is all, not what was said, not who was talkin'. I piled off my horse — I didn't know what to do scarcely. It was awful quiet when I got into those rocks. It was powerful dark. If I hadn't stumbled over Grounds I probably wouldn't of known he was there."

"How did you know — I mean, know it was him?"

"Scratched a match."

"Some surprised, wasn't you?"

"I was terrified."

"But you got your horse and packed him off."

"I couldn't just leave him like he was a piece of waste paper!"

"No skin off your nose. You hadn't never seen him till a couple hours before."

She give me a careful look. "You don't believe that?"

"I'm trying to get at the facts," I said. "If a jury ever gets called in on this —"

"Well . . . I didn't just go fetch my horse. I heard talking again when I got back to the pens. Before it had seemed to be off towards the house . . . like where I found Grounds maybe. This talk was coming from behind the corrals. Two men it sounded like, arguin' . . . I think one was Brace. He was pretty excited."

Probably Brace and the kid. I said as much,

adding, “Ivory wouldn’t let them sleep in the house.” It come over me then. The first voices, the ones that had pulled her into the rocks, was the same ones I’d heard back at the house — Grounds and whoever had used that knife.

I said, “You better not tell no one else about this.”

She went still, darkly staring. Then her jaw dropped a little. Some of the color leached out of her cheeks. “You mean — ?”

“That feller might get the idea you could name him. Might make up his mind not to take any chances.” I considered her grimly. “I think you’d be smart to get the hell out of here.”

She got that stubborn look back on her face. “All right,” I said, “stay if you got to, but at least keep away from the house.”

“They’ll know he didn’t walk off by himself!”

“You’d of been a heap smarter to have thought of that sooner.” I swore then, disgusted. Brace or Lupita. Either one of them could of killed him. From the way Dimity had curled back her lip when I had mentioned Fred’s wife it was plain there wasn’t no love lost there. And Brace . . .

I remembered something else. The way he had looked stepping around that corpse, and my thinking how unlikely it was he should miss stumbling into a thing he didn’t know was there. And her telling me now about him sounding excited. He’d be excited all right if, in the flare of that match, he’d seen her crouched over a dead body — her that had run him into that cactus.

He was weasel enough to use it, too.

"Stay here," I said, "and —"

She never let me finish. Shoulders back and jaw hitched up, she come right out with it. "I'm goin' back with you."

"Christ," I snarled. "You want to get yourself killed!" She paled again but she didn't back off. "I can't put my life ahead of Fred's need."

"Don't talk like a fool!" I seen her eyes flatten out. I said, more reasonable, "What the hell can you do?"

"I don't know, but I can try. If I can just make them see there's no loot to squabble over. . . ."

Man might as well argue with the shadow of death.

XVI

I caught up a horse for her, saddled it. We started.

She hadn't spoke a word since. I hadn't, neither, but there was plenty of words locked back of my teeth. About the worst thing she could do was go back there, deliberately putting her life in my hands. For that's what it come to. Making me responsible, compelling me to help whether I was minded to or not.

It was blackmail, slicker than slobbers.

Straightaway she'd seen I wasn't taking hold of that "No plunder" foolishness. So she'd pegged me for tough, a gunhung drifter, a main chance bravo, light on scruples and long on greed. She'd likely been plenty acquainted with such in the time she had spent on this place with Jake Gauze.

I've said she was smart. She was proving it now; a country girl who walked and talked and rode like a man but thought with the crossgrained mind of a witch. Hell — what else could I think, knowing what she was up to? She wanted Fred helped and didn't care who she got killed in the process.

A harsh judgment, sure — but no worse than she'd give me. Greed, she figured, would suck a man into anything. She was so convinced she didn't even look around.

I was powerful minded to upset her calculations, if only to by God prove that she was wrong. Serve her right if I yanked the grulla's head around and rode straight out of this jackpot! She pegged me right, you'll say, or I'd have done it.

Well, I didn't.

It was two hours to noon and hotter than a blister when we rode through the slot and come up to Fred's corrals with nothing between us and the house but them rocks.

She swung out of her saddle. Still mad, I followed suit. I was in a ringy mood and both them caballos knowed it. Stripping off the gear I choused them into the nearest pen, and took after her. They ought to be rubbed down and cooled out. Knowing this didn't improve my temper, but I had no time to fool with them. She was off through the rocks like a bat out of Carlsbad.

Cort Brace in his socks was setting on the front porch and she was climbing the steps when I come in sight of her. She had more guts than you could hang on a fencepost. She went straight on in.

I paused on the steps to wipe the sweat off my hands. "Ivory picked up the guns?"

Brace, hiding his hate, shook his head.

"Pretty sure, eh?"

Something curled like smoke behind the gambler's stare. My eyes let go of him then and I went in.

All the rest of them was there, hunkered like buzzards round a broken-legged skunk, the skunk in this picture, of course, being Fred. His whiskered jaw was sunk on his chest and the quiet would of stuffed a place ten times as big. Everyone else had their stares on the girl. She had her back to the door. I couldn't see her face but I could see Ivory fine.

He said, "I don't give a damn who slit his throat. What I want to know is why you moved him."

"I already told you why," Dimity said. "He was dead. So I buried him. Ain't that reason enough?"

"Not for me," Ivory growled. "You claim he ate with you last night. You claim he rode up here to tell old Jake there never was no treasure, that him and Zwing Hunt made the whole thing up." Considering her, still with that bullypuss grin, he said in a easy teasing way, "I'll put it to you straight. Even if there wasn't no plunder, you think a guy like him would come clean up from Texas on a fool deal like that?"

"All I know is what he said."

The quiet come back.

"You going to stick with that story?"

"It's not a story. It's the truth."

Ivory said with a trace of impatience, "The truth as you know it, mebbe. What'd he say about the map Hunt made when he was dyin' back there in Santone?"

"Never mentioned a map. He said the whole thing was a joke him and Hunt made up for laughs."

"He may of told that to you; he knew a sight better than to try it on Jake. I tell you, girl, I've checked this out. Curly Bill did sack Matamoras. They come out of Mexico with two four-horse wagons loaded with plunder. From a bank they stuck up in Monterey they got two bulgin' gunny sacks crammed with money and a cigar box full of diamonds. From the cathedral at Matamoras they carted off full-length life-size figures of Christ and the Virgin Mary . . . *solid gold*. I talked with the priests.

"Now listen to what Zwing Hunt told about it. This come straight from his uncle. 'One of our men who'd been shot in that bank job kicked off at Davis Mountain and we planted him by Silver Spring. Five hundred dollars in gold was his cut. He'd damn well risked his life for that money so we buried it with him. It's in a tin can at the head of his grave.' "

Brace, who'd got up and was standing in the door, was pretty near drooling. His eyes stuck out like knots on a stick. Oakes hadn't moved. Lupita's stare was bright as brass, and the kid had both ears out at least a foot and forty inches.

I stepped against the wall trying to catch

Dimity's look and Ivory, like he was her big brother, said, "So you see that pins it down pretty definite. Look outside and what do you see? Silver Spring and that mountain back of it." His bold stare slanched a glance at Fred where the old coot sat like he was hacked out of wood, and come back to me with a knowing wink.

Dimity said, more stubborn than ever, "That doesn't change anything. You knew this the same as Fred. What nobody knew — except Curly Bill, maybe-was that Grounds and Hunt made it up for a joke. You've got Grounds' word for it."

Brace scowled. "Grounds is dead."

"That's right," Ivory smiled. "All we've really got, ma'am, is your words that Grounds come up here to set old Jake straight, which make about as much sense as Jake, here, thinkin' he can hog the whole works."

They all started talking at once then. They made enough noise for a convention of coyotes. When they reached for fresh breaths, Ivory, cutting in, said, "If I'm allowed a suggestion, how's about the women rustlin' up a little grub? Shouting and swearing won't butter no parsnips."

Dimity cried, "This whole thing's ridiculous!"

"Not much point to it," Ivory said, "when all you got to do is go out there and dig."

That fetched to their faces some pretty startled looks. Kid said, "Where?"

"Well, myself I'd favor spadin' up around that

spring." Ivory grinned with open amusement. "If the dead man's there with his can of gold I would say Hunt pretty well knew what he was oratin' about." He settled back with a chuckle. "What do you think, Jake?"

If ever I seen hate it was on Fred's face then.

Ivory laughed.

The girls went off into the kitchen part. I said, "Hunt must've left some kind of instructions."

"He's supposed to've wrote out some. You can find as many different versions as maps. I talked to the uncle," Ivory said, smiling. "That Mexican trip come ahead of the Skeleton Canyon rub-outs, the way I got it from him. That last bunch of smugglers the gang wiped out was really loaded. Big mule train. Supposed to been ninety thousand in Mex'kin money and thirty-nine bars of gold. They buried this by three live oaks at the mouth of Skeleton Canyon.

"Few days later — still according to Zwing's uncle — Hunt and Grounds fetched a wagon driven by a Mex and moved this swag to the pit already half filled with the loot they'd brought up out of the south. Teamster was shot and dumped in on top. They burned the wagon."

Brace with a glassy look was rubbing at the soreness them cactuses put in him. Alamagordo scowled.

"By the uncle's tell," Ivory's tone turned gruff, "on this map Hunt made he set down in positions the mountain, the springs, the place where they burnt the wagon, a rock with two crosses and an X for the spot where the plunder is buried." With his grin spreading out he said bland as butter, "Jake has the map. Why not get him to give you a look at it?"

Oakes seemed to settle deeper into his clothes and all the lines of his face run together. He was trapped and he knowed it, and finally pushed himself up. Not looking at nobody he mumbled, "I'll git it."

Like something on strings he stepped around the table. Brace, jumping up, said, "I'll go with him."

Ivory's eyes pushed him back. "Jake's not about to run out on his friends."

He could of said *Where would he run to?* What he actually added across that cold grin was, "Not while we got Dimity Hale."

Fred tried hard but you could see him wilt. He might of carried all the weight of the world on his shoulders, his steps was that shaky. Lupita, stirring something at the stove, twisted her head to eye the whipped look of him shambling past. He mumbled at Dimity. I seen her startled face when she turned. She looked about to argue. He muttered again. She backed off out of sight. A moment later her arm come out and something passed from her hand into his.

Oakes come back and dropped the dog-eared folds of a paper on the table. Brace snatched it up, the kid at his elbow. I didn't go over, didn't even watch them smooth it out against the wood. I was staring at Ivory, grudgingly giving him the respect that was his due.

How could he have known? He couldn't, of course; it had to be a guess. But a man who could guess like that. . . . His eyes laughed.

"This don't help too much," Brace said, looking up. He was plainly disappointed. The kid said, ugly, "There ain't no dimensions."

Ivory nodded. "Didn't figure there would be. Stood to reason. Jake, if it had been so simple as that, would of had it and flown. Hunt give his uncle a few extra notions that wasn't put down as a part of that map. He said the gang played poker in a cave on Davis Mountain — said they bathed in the waterfall and that with glasses they could see from the mountain clean into New Mexico."

"Ain't no waterfall here," Brace said in a nettled whine. He looked to hold Ivory personally responsible.

Ivory grinned. "When you go after treasure what you need's imagination. That's why Jake ain't done no better than he has."

They stared at him, angered, then turned to glare at Oakes. "I bet," the kid said, "this ain't even the place! I never heard of no Davis Mountain!"

"I expect we'll find out about that when you dig."

The gambler and the kid was still grumbling over Hunt's map when the gaff in them words begun to scratch Brace. He jerked up his face in a glowering stare. "Ain't you goin' to be diggin' too?"

"Oh," Ivory smiled with his usual offhand easy assurance, "I might turn over a shovelful mebbe. Any proper alliance has a place for everyone; a simple matter of talents. A place for lookers, a place for diggers —"

"And what," the kid growled, "do you figger to be doin' while the rest of us is sweatin'?"

"Using the talent I'm contributing, of course."

"And what would that be?" Lupita asked from the kitchen.

Ivory put up a finger and tapped his head. "Imagination."

"It sure has brought you a far piece, Fi—"

"Thank you." He bowed with a audacious flourish.

Fred was keeping out of this. Brace looked affronted. "If that means," the kid rasped, "you'll stand around doin' nothin'."

"Somebody's got to be boss," I said. "So long as we're all getting a chunk of what's found."

"All that freely contribute," Ivory coolly said. "There's obviously got to be some basis for shares. Brace and the kid, here, with picks and shovels. Jake's furnishing the map and . . . other particulars. Farsom his pistol." His look, brightly amused, passed on to Fred's wife. "And what will you be furnishing, my dear?"

"You son of a bitch!" Lupita said whitely.

"Tsk, tsk," Ivory clucked. "Such talk from a lady."

I got up from my chair. Not a pair of eyes shifted. I stepped around Fred and tramped off to my room, remembering the look of her when Oakes had told Ivory Grounds had been the only man still afoot actually to know where the plunder was planted.

I went in, shut the door, and shoved a hand under the bureau. Pure carelessness; I might of pushed into the fangs of a rattler. Way it turned out there wasn't anything under that wood but my hand. Like Billy Grounds, the knife was gone.

I don't know how long I stood there. When I got back they had the grub on the table, the smells of it curling up off the plates in a stillness that suddenly caught at my notice.

Brace was having some trouble with his breathing. The kid's cheeks was flushed. He come onto his feet looking meaner than gar soup. "How much," he snarled, slamming his words into Fred, "did they lift off that mule train of smugglers?"

"Ask his wife," Ivory said. "She was part of that train — the only one that got away. The 'stripling'." He laughed at Fred's look. "Lupita Garcia, the old Don's daughter."

XVII

That sure as hell tore it, far as Fred was concerned.

It was enough to knock anybody off his perch, to get told in such fashion his wife was the daughter of a guy he'd helped murder — and no telling how many more of her kin. I thought to Betsy he would bust his surcingle. His face begun to bulge. I moved in quick, figuring to get hold of him before he done her a mortal hurt.

Ivory, eyeing him slanchways, chuckled. "Jake won't touch her. Be same as admitting he fixed Grounds' clock."

I wasn't too sure about that, thinking to myself he might be selling Fred short, but it soon become evident he had yanked the right string. By degrees Oakes sagged back into his clothes. The wild look finally quit his face. He dropped onto the bench like a man with the ague.

Lupita, while the rest of us was staring at Fred, had time enough to iron out her looks, and done it. Most of what Ivory had said made the kind of hard sense a feller couldn't get around, tying in so many of the things that had stumped me and that maybe had been gnawing at Fred off and on. It was her had killed Grounds. I was sure of that now.

You had to admire her gall. She done what she could. Looking scornful at all of us she passed Brace the meat and, with her lip curled back, said, "What kind of yarn have you figured out for Flick?"

Ivory flashed his teeth, helped himself to the hashed browns and reached across for the plate Brace held. "Long as Farsom and me understand each other there's no point proddin' up facts that might embarrass him."

That there was mighty few facts of that sort to be prodded made no difference at all. By such a slick gabble of words he had crippled opposition, making it appear him and me was buen amigos, that anyone figuring to put a spoke in his wheel would have me to reckon with.

Without promising a thing, he'd got us so worked up — so filled with frustrating suspicions, there was hardly a chance we'd get together against him. Covert glances was passing around thick as bugs when Fred said, gruff, through the squirmy quiet, "What you figger on doin' if diggin' around that spring don't turn up nothin'?"

"You better just hope it don't come to that."

The stillness got thicker. You could tell by his look Ivory wasn't about to stand for much foolishness.

Dimity from the first had hardly been more than picking at her food. I seen her chin come up, and dug eyes hard into her trying to head it off. She said bound and determined, "If you'd half the sense God give to a gopher you'd know mighty well if there'd been anything around Fred would of had it dug up and spent long ago!"

Ivory grinned.

Brace growled, "Fred ain't the spendin' kind."

And Fred himself, prodded finally into speech, heaved another bitter sigh, grumbling, "Let's git on with it."

He pushed up from the table, the kid and Brace following. Lupita's look stayed fixed to her plate; but Dimity, coming off the bench, bewilderedly cried, "You surely ain't serious? . . ."

"I expect," Ivory said, "Grounds found it so." His glance picked up Fred's wife. "You got anything more to contribute?"

She watched him sullenly, eyes twin pools of seething hate. At the door Brace twisted his face to whine, "You makin' me dig without no boots?"

"You can swing the pick."

Stepping over to the stove, never turning his back, Ivory pushed in Brace's boots and set the lids back on. He shoved the point of Brace's knife into the joint of the oven, snapping off half the blade, tossing Lupita what was left in his hand. "I can break a arm or a leg just as easy." Motioning me ahead of him he stepped onto the porch.

But Dimity wouldn't leave it there. She had to come storming after him. It scared me — and I guess Fred too, when she grabbed Ivory's arm.

Must of been the one he'd trained for his gun work. White as chalk he snatched it out of her grip and come clean around like a shot-stung bear. I tell you, by God, he looked plumb loco with the spit fuzzin' out around them teeth and his eyes blazing wild. I reckoned for sure he would knock her down, and I couldn't of moved to save my soul.

Oakes, too, stood froze and, like the rest of them, about as much help as a .22 cartridge in a twelve-gauge gun.

Ivory hauled a deep breath. Some of the stiffness let go. Terrible quiet he said, "Never touch me again. Never put your hands on me."

We stood there like fools with them eyes biting into us.

With a bark of a laugh he motioned us on. My throat was so dry I couldn't spit even.

Like I mentioned before, no Davis Mountains was on any map of this country I'd looked at. There was some named Davis over in West Texas, but nothing about them tallied with Hunt's story. I'd been all through them. No waterfalls over there. Far as that went there was none around here, though Fred's wife had called this place Silver Springs and right off had told me it was in the Davis Mountains.

Fred rounded up a shovel and a oak-handled

pick and Brace and the kid squared off and went to digging. I stood in the shade of a cottonwood with Ivory and watched Fred hunker with his back to a rock. He looked as near natural as I'd ever seen him.

It must have been powerful hot working out in that sun with all the rock-trapped heat swirling round, but for the first hour or so them boys kept hard at it. When they finally knocked off to get some ginger back into them Brace, red as fire, flopped flat on his belly, plopping his face right into the spring.

"Better go easy on that," I said.

The kid come out of his soggy shirt and Brace, getting up with the front of him dripping, declared, "At this rate, by Gawd, we're like to be here till Christmas!"

I said, peering at Oakes, "You sure this is the place?"

Looked like his mind was a million miles away, squatting there dribbling dirt through his fingers.

"It's the place," Ivory nodded.

Brace swore, scowling at Fred. "An' who's to say he ain't already been dug up?"

"Maybe Dimity's right," I said.

"And maybe she figures to save it for Fred." Ivory's look toughened. "Get on with your digging."

The kid spit on his hands. "I'll have a go at that pick." He took a hard look around like he was trying to discover the best place to begin at.

They had already worked clean around the spring.

Steps sounded back of us. It was Dimity Hale and behind her, coming through the rocks, was Lupita. Alamagordo, scowling, asked if she had any ideas on the subject. Fred's wife said, "You're not deep enough. Put a little muscle in it."

The kid got down in the pit, spit again on his hands, begun swinging that pick like he was going for China. Ten minutes later while he was resting his strength, Brace, working back of him, shoveled out some bones. Ivory, scrambling down, squatted over them.

"Chest bones," he grinned, lifting one to show us, whacking the earth from it. His glance come up with a plain satisfaction that curled into a scowl as Lupita's hard stare drew his look back and down. Out of the shoveled-away dirt he picked a moldering length that must have come off a leg.

Didn't take no crystal ball to know a thing of that kind wouldn't be mixed in with ribs without this ground had been stirred up before. His look found Fred. He got out of the pit. As Oakes come to his feet Ivory shoved the bone hard against Fred's breast. "Old man, you better talk fast," he said.

Fred shrunk back, waggling his head. Wouldn't of surprised me none if Ivory'd gone to beating him with it. Then Dimity run up, pushing reckless between them. Eyes blazing, she cried, "You ought to be ashamed, bullying a man old enough to be your father!"

Ivory glared. Dropping the bone he spun around, the leap of his glance searing Brace and the kid. "See if you can turn up that can!" he snarled.

The gambler wiped his streaming face. The kid took the shovel and started poking around, turning over the broken dirt, scraping through it. Oakes let Dimity lead him off into the shade. He appeared more stunned than scairt or guilty with his jaw hanging open and his shambling steps. I seen his wife and Brace exchange quick looks as Ivory, scowling, jumped into the pit and commenced impatiently to scuff around with his boots.

Then the kid, bitterly swearing, reached down and come up with a bent and rusted tin that any fool could see had once been a can like the kind they had buried full of gold when the guy was planted. You could see plain enough there was no gold in it now.

We all looked at Fred as the piece of scabrous metal thudded harsh beside his feet. The eyes jumped around in his cheeks like dying fishes. Even Dimity looked shaken.

"Tomorrow," Ivory said, "you're going to show us where you put it."

XVIII

This was one of the things about Ivory that scared you — his uncanny habit of cutting straight to the facts. He'd dig up these remarks that first rattle out of his mouth looked loco, and next thing you know we was seeing the God's awful truth of them. Like Fred, and Hunt's map. Like Lupita being the daughter of that murdered boss smuggler. She was one, by grab, I figured to swap words with. But I could see getting to do it wasn't going to be like falling off no log.

One of the things I wanted to know was what she had got out of Grounds before she had put that knife to his throat. Was it her had brought him here? I wanted to know too where that knife was now, but more than everything else I wondered why Ivory had left this bunch of galoots heeled. Worked up like we was it seemed a crazy damn risk he hadn't needed to take.

Fred I noticed, though he looked like a man stumbling around in his sleep, managed handily to stay within reach of the big man's stare. Part of the time, while supper was getting, Dimity was off with Fred's wife out of sight, but while I could see her she never opened her mouth.

After we had got the grub stowed away — and I doubt if anybody knowed or cared what they was putting into them, the whole shebang set around in the glare of that big front room like they was holding a wake or a seeance or something. And every time I looked at the girl she was staring at Fred like a dying calf. She looked worse than he did.

Wasn't nobody doing any great amount of talking. Brace mostly looked at his bootless feet. I guess all of us was thinking more or less about that plunder which — according to Ivory — Fred would be showing us first thing tomorrow, wondering maybe if he'd called the turn again. Probably wondering too if there would be any chance of getting Fred off to himself for a little bit.

Some such notion may have been gnawing Fred because when Ivory, stretching, finally quit his chair, Fred shot up like he couldn't do it quick enough. "I been thinkin'," he said to me, "if you got no objections, I'd as lief spend the night in that back room with you."

Alamagordo stared. Ivory showed his sour grin. Lupita's lips come together like the jaws of a trap. Fred's eyes frittered around not looking at nobody when Ivory took off his hat and said slyly, "Ain't nervous, are you?"

"Hell," Brace said, "I don't mind settin' up with him."

Ivory chuckled. "Sure, he'll take care of you. If

it'll make you feel better you could leave your door open." Then he looked at the kid. "I'll leave mine open too, and —" his glance picked up Fred's wife, "be a good idea if you left one of these lamps lit."

Brace turned ringy. The kid's lips cracked away from his teeth and a oily shine come over Fred's cheeks.

"What are you trying to do," Dimity cried, "scare him to death?"

Ivory's stare come up off his hat. "No call to talk rough. If there's one thing all of us share in this place it's the high regard we got for ol' Jake. Ain't that right, pardner?"

Oakes' stooped shape stiffened piece by piece. He had enough sense to keep the fright off his face, enough savvy not to beg, but it was there. You could smell it.

Dimity's mouth came apart and you could read in her eyes she suddenly knew what Fred and all the rest of us had saw: that without some kind of miracle popped up she was staring at a man who could mighty soon be dead.

Now was the time, if he ever meant to do it, for him to come straight out and make the best deal he could with whatever information he'd been hugging to himself. But all he done was stand there.

The look of that girl got to be too much for me.

"I ain't sleepy," I said. "Go on and get your rest, Fred. I'll be settin' right here. Nobody's goin' to bother you."

There was a pretty good chance, when you come right down to it, I might be setting there forever. Though I called myself seven kinds of a fool, the look I got from Dimity spread a tight warm glow inside me.

She went off to bed. Lupita, wheeling into the hall after her, slipped me a kind of bullypuss stare; then the rest of them, milling, commenced straggling away. I turned my back, knowing Ivory was watching, and went around snuffing lamps till there was only one left. This I picked up, and turning it low, set it under the planks of that big stripped table where its funnel of light, fanning out across the floor, filled the length of the hall with a dim lemon glow.

Now the upper half of the front room was dark. I pulled Fred's chair off to one side and stood there a minute, uncomfortably aware of that open porch door. The far right corner of the room had no window. I dragged the chair over there.

This put a wall to my back, door and window off to the left of me, table to my right and the hall dead ahead. But the shine of that lamp come straight at my eyes. I went back, turning one of the benches over.

Now my chair was in shadow. Fred's door was open; Ivory's, too, but if anyone stepped into the hall I could see them. I bent by the table, turned the lamp down some more, then went back to my chair.

I wiped the sweat off my face. Ivory's light went out.

The place quieted down. Sounds drifted in from the night, the chirk of crickets, the cry of an owl. Twice in the next hour I caught myself nodding. You might think with all I had on my mind the last think I'd have to watch out for was sleep, but I'd got none last night, I'd fought those broncs all day yesterday; it was beginning to catch up with me.

The next time I pulled the chin off my chest there wasn't a snort or a snore, not even the shriek of a settling timber. There was no sound outside, and that wasn't natural.

I took hold of my pistol.

The quiet got so loud it put a ache in my ears. I could see the length of the hall and there wasn't no door in that end of the house — nothing going outside, I mean; but Ivory's room had a window. He had used it last night . . . was he using it now? Which room was Dimity's? And what about that kid? Was Fred still in bed?

Questions — my damn head was full of them. The back door, I remembered, opened out of the kitchen, the alcove part I couldn't see from my chair. Maybe, I thought, I'd better look in Fred's room, if only to make certain he was still there and breathing.

I got out of the chair, carefully working the kinks from my neck and shoulders, standing there then with the gun in my hand. I eased out of my boots, finally setting them down, and looked a long time into that lamp lighted hall. Two things I could do: go look in Fred's room or stay right where I was. Before I done anything something moved in the kitchen with a Indian stealth; more a hunch, I guess, than any definite sound. I was pretty near scairt to twist my head, but I done it.

And saw not one thing I hadn't looked at before.

Just the same there was something. The lampflame was climbing up one side of the glass and a suction of air was running over my feet. Like a door had been opened.

Hardest thing I ever done was go out in that kitchen. Door was open, all right — clean back against the wall. Maybe this was what had roused me. If it had been open very long the flame in that lamp would have blackened the chimney.

You're right — I was stalling. Maybe any guy would that had a lick of sense. One of this bunch, while I'd been pounding my ear, had slipped outside . . . or was this what they wanted me to think? Some hoax set up to get me out of the house? Brace, or that kid, might not be so cute, but Ivory could have rigged it. And so could Fred's wife. I could see plain enough no matter what I done would probably be the wrong thing.

The need to look into that hall overpowered me, or maybe it was Dimity that turned me around. I was already moving when a snaggle of whispers stopped me cold in my tracks. Every hair on my scalp stood up and I spun, gun lifting, to stare into the night.

Too black to see, but there was somebody out there. Two of them, anyways. One was furious, apparently threatening, savagely angry. There was whispers again, the sounds of a scuffle, the crack of a hand flat and hard against flesh.

I went out, crouched low, trying to get the shapes of them against that murky sky. The dark bulk of the canyon wall was too near. Somebody gasped. There was a flutter of motion. Booted feet beat a clatterous retreat through loose shale. I fired into the racket, no yell frittering back.

Pistol flame jumped from the house's far corner, the whine of that bullet singing bitterly close. No time for thinking. I went down on one knee, drove two shots at the flash. Somebody screamed. I leaped up and run toward him, cursing, gun lifted.

He was down, all right. I could see the dark blotch of him. I pulled up, brassy mouthed, fighting vomit, the ragged thud of my heart the loudest sound in all that clamor. The runner had hid himself in the confusion, the night was suddenly shouting with eyes.

I backed off, fading away from that place, anxious and dreading what I'd find in the house, knowing I'd better get in there quick. No good hunting for the one that hadn't run. I cut in toward the kitchen, hearing the gabble of voices, still hearing my heart, too. The back door was open. I went in fast.

Dimity, in the hall, come around at one swipe,

her eyes big as sauce pans. She was dressed and standing not a arm's length from Ivory who, though bare to the waist, had a gun in his fist. I kept hold of mine, too.

We peered at each other while the quietness piled up, Ivory finally breaking it. "You do all that shootin'?"

I sloshed into my boots, bent and got the lamp out from under the table. Eyeing Fred's closed door I twirled up the wick. "He's gettin' his clothes on," Dimity said.

It didn't strike me at once what a odd thing it was that Fred, of all people, should have peeled off for bed. I made a bet with myself that nobody else had. Dimity's eyes, narrowing, darkened. "I thought you were going to stay in that chair."

"Seems a lot of folks did. Where's the rest of this outfit?" I shoved my glance at Ivory.

He stared, eyes flattening, hefting his gun. "You sound kind of proddy."

I give him both barrels, blunt enough to stop clocks. "There's a jasper outside won't be wantin' no breakfast. There was two others out there I didn't catch up with."

His look come full open. I heard Dimity gasp. One of the shut doors cracked, Fred's wife popping her head out. "You damn fools going to caterwaul all night?"

Shoving past Ivory I got a fistfull of night rail, hauling her out where we could all have a squint at her. She come scratching and swearing, looking madder than hops.

I slammed her into the wall. "You goin' to talk, by God, or have I got to rip it off you?"

Even Ivory looked startled. You could tell by the fit of it she had all her clothes on.

Her eyes was like daggers. She slanched her look at Fred who had just that minute come up. "You going to let this bastard insult me?"

"Could he?" Fred said.

"All right," she snapped, rounding back on me, "if a girl has to go she's got to, don't she?"

Dimity's cheeks fired.

Ivory smiled, watching us. "Who was with you?"

"No —"

"Powerful lot of mutterin'," I said. "You always wrassle with yourself when you step out to squat?"

She went up in smoke. There was blood on my cheeks when they dragged her off. She called me every damn name she could put tongue to.

"Someone," I said, when she run out of breath, "took off like a twister. Then a gun by the corner of the house opened up — pretty near had my name on it, too! I fired at the flash. You want to go have a look at him?"

"Bound to be either Brace," Fred said, "or that kid."

"They bed down in the house?"

Ivory shook his head, switched his look to Lupita. "You want to sing a little now?"

"It was Brace," she said sullenly. "He knew who I was — it was him put me up to marryin'

Jake. He's been at me to get his hands on that map."

You couldn't tell what Fred thought. I figured about a quarter of what she said might be true. "And tonight?" Ivory purred, "what'd he want with you tonight?"

The red lips curled. "That crystal ball of yours broke down?"

He cracked her across the face so hard her head banged into the door frame. Part of her hair come down, the marks of his fingers showing livid on her skin.

You'd of thought after that she would have called it a day, but all he'd done was turn her more wild. Her nostrils flared like a trumpeting horse. "You son of a bitch!" she cried, tearing into him. She made a grab for his pistol and he struck her again — this time with the barrel of it. She went legs over elbows, fetching up in a heap.

She come onto one knee. I seen the blood mixed into the spittle on her chin, but she had guts — by God, you had to give her that. She wasn't one to let a little hurting cramp her style. "What's the matter, mister?" she snapped at me. "You glued there or somethin'?"

I couldn't get enough wet in my gullet to swaller.

"Never mind!" she snarled, and got onto her feet with that hair every whichway, eyes burning out of it. She hawked up a frog and spit it square in his face. "You been blowed up so much by them pelados you run with I guess you think, Fisher, you really are a king. Hell, you'll cut just the same as any other two-legged bastard!"

I seen the flash of a knife as she flung herself at him. Flame jumped from his fist. She run right into it.

XIX

Once a thing's over a man can generally figure what he ought to done different, and it was that way with me. Perhaps Fred's wife had used up her luck getting clear of that Skeleton Canyon massacre. Maybe her course was laid out and decided before ever she'd come to Silver Spring but I couldn't help thinking if I'd been a shade quicker, or jumped that devil when she first lit into him, I wouldn't be feeling quite so draggle-tail mean.

With the smoke whimmerin' round through them clattering echoes we stood like bent sticks, scarce breathing, frozen-eyed, hamstrung by the truths confronting us.

Wasn't a man in that room hadn't heard of King Fisher, or could doubt this was him now she'd put the name to him. The fancy clothes, the slick deadly feel of him — that grin and the gun, had figured too bright in things told round the cow camps. He rated with Thompson and John Wesley Hardin, a gun slamming galoot who killed without quarter — we had the truth of that, too.

We knew — or anyways I did — it was Brace outside that had been doing the jawing, that lit out through the shale the minute I'd showed. We had Lupita's word for it, and this put the kid at the corner of the house. I hadn't a doubt it was him we would find there. I was more concerned now to discover where Brace was.

"Hold up," Fisher growled as I started for the porch. "Where you off to?"

"Brace," I grumbled over a shoulder.

"I'm givin' the orders here," Fisher said. "You want to stay healthy you better remember it." His eyes was like a pair of baked marbles. With that gun in his fist I hadn't much choice. "Stop right where you are," he said, and I done it.

Sure I had a gun in my hand. He grinned when he saw me reluctantly let go of it. His glance slanched over Fred and the girl. "Pretty soon Jake's going to dig up that plunder. Just to make sure we all know where we're at I'm dabbin' a loop round this Hale filly's neck."

When first light spread its sheep's wool gray behind that jagged rim to the east Fisher levered himself up out of the chair. Walking past Dimity he got hold of the rope, flipping the loose end of it over a rafter, hauling in slack till he had her right under it. He give a couple of tugs that fetched her onto her toes, eyes weighing Fred — watching me even more before, thinly grinning, he let go of enough to let her heels come back down. "Expect you know what'll happen if things don't come off accordin' to Hoyle."

He was all through fooling. Any nump could see that.

First thing he'd done after getting the noose round her was to take Fred's pistol and then lift hers, thrusting them into the pockets of his coat. He broke the blade of Lupita's dropped knife, told Fred to find a shovel and put her under ground — as though getting her out of sight was like to fix anything.

With her over his shoulder Fred stumbled out. Taking up the lamp I followed. Like a dog on a leash Dimity came after, Fisher, with the guns, bringing up the rear.

A change had set in. It was like a smell on the air.

The West in its time had managed to live with a heap of things, some of them violent, a few downright bad. But no part I'd heard tell of had so far been able to swaller a killed woman. What had happened to Lupita was gnawing pretty sharp. Like the scratch of sand it stayed harsh in our thinking, each guarded look, every breath we drew, isolating Fisher, setting us against him as nothing else could.

He seen it, too. It was why he'd disarmed us, it was back of him putting that rope on Dimity. He'd had to have some way to keep us in line but he sure didn't look to be putting much trust in it. His stare jumped around like a boxful of crickets.

Killing that woman kept chewing on him. He

couldn't forget it. When we come to that corner and didn't find the kid I thought for a minute he would bust his britches.

Maybe I looked as flabbergasted as I felt. Fred was the only one that didn't seem bothered. He stood with his wife hunched over one shoulder and looked like he hadn't no more mind than an idiot.

Fisher snarled, waving his pistol. "Git that lamp down where we can see somethin'!"

"Here's where he stood," I said, pointing out the marks. There was a scuffed place just past them. I pointed again. "Looks like blood."

Fisher poked out a finger, sniffed it and nodded. "Guess you knocked him down, all right." His glance, weighing Dimity, moved on to Fred. "Hell," I said, "they ain't been out of your sight."

He eyed me a while, stabbed a squint at the sky. "Take a look in the bunkhouse."

We trailed through the rocks filled with our thinking. The shovel they'd used to put Grounds away stood against the poles of the nearest corral. Fisher tossed it at Fred, motioning me on.

The bunkhouse was dark. Packing that lamp like I was, and no pistol, I expected any minute to get shot clean loose of my everlasting soul, but nothing happened. We come up to the place. I kicked open the door.

No sign of the kid. But Brace was there, all shivers and shakes.

"On your feet!" Fisher barked.

Eyes rolling, Brace come out of his blanket.

"All right," Fisher said. "What'd you do with him?"

"Never touched the little bastard — as Gawd's my witness he was gone when I got there!"

"Gone where?"

Damn fool was so scairt you could hear his teeth clacking. "C-c-leared out, I guess — your horse is g-g-gone, too."

Fisher spun Dimity round and shoved her out through the door. At the corrals the truth of what Brace said was apparent. The only horse there was Fred's big grulla. He tromped up to us, nickering, put his head over the poles.

I switched the lamp to my other hand. Fisher's look was black as thunder. "All right, Brace. You pile on this mouse and go fetch in those broncs Jake's been holdin'."

"Broncs?" Brace quavered. "What b-b-broncs?"

"You'll find 'em. Just foller your nose. And don't be all night." Fisher's look turned impatient.

Brace's rabbity face was covered with sweat. Great drops stood out on his narrow-boned cheeks. His Adam's apple worked like the float on a troutline. "B-but —"

"Look!" Fisher growled. "Do this right and I'll take care of you."

Brace swallowed noisily. Swallowed again.

"Jump, God damn you!" Fisher cried, tipping his gun up.

With a frightened squawk Brace went through the poles. Fisher waved Dimity and me toward the sound of Fred's digging.

And now here we was, turning over thought we'd been through a hundred times while day come bumbling towards us out of the night. Fred hadn't spoke all the time we was waiting. Dimity's eyes was like burns in a bed sheet. She finally roused to tell Fisher wearily, "The only thing Fred's dug up is post holes."

Fisher's face showed his scorn.

I said, "But what if she's right? What if there ain't no goddam plunder?"

"What's he got all them pack saddles for?"

The stillness filled with our unspoken fears. Beyond the east window the darkness curdled, become gray as fog. Stringers of it swirled across the porch and pearl gray floating puffs of it swooped in to curl around us like the gnawing of our thoughts.

Fisher said, "Here they come," and the gulch was loud with the racket of horses.

XX

Through everything else — even the cold shaking shivers of what I felt for the girl, I kept going back to what had happened at the corner of the house. There was a fuzziness there, black sliding into black, beyond the bright burst of that muzzle flash. It was the kid right enough — nobody else showed hurt, and I'd seen the dark blotch of him there on the ground.

We'd found blood, and then boot marks. Still it kept nipping me . . . something unfinished, something pushed aside, lost in a welter of more striking impressions. That kid wasn't tough, he'd only wanted to be, and the light had been bad. If all I'd done was wing him he would of sure enough bolted soon's I went in the house. With Fisher's horse gone there wasn't much else a man could think.

Brace's reedy voice come out of the murk.

"Come in," Fisher growled.

The tinhorn showed up, flapping over the porch in what was left of his socks. His eyes goggled round. He sleeved the drip off his chin. "I didn't g-git all of 'em . . ." He run a hand round his collar. "S-some got away but what I got is shut up in them p-pens."

"You done fine," Fisher nodded. He put his pistol away, hard stare drilling Fred.

Fred's look cringed away. He worked his jaw up and down. When the words finally come you'd of thought they'd been hauled all the way up from China. "I'm ready."

Fisher, grinning, took hold of the rope. I grabbed at his arm. "You figurin'," I said, "to leave her tied to that rafter?"

"You got a better way to keep him in line?"

Fred said, husky, "I won't make you no trouble."

"I will," I said, "if you don't git that rope off her."

His look banged into my face like a fist. I don't know why he didn't shoot me right then. The whole top half of him swelled. He jerked himself loose and rared back like a scorpion, hand hooked to pounce for the grips of his pistol. His stare in that quiet was like slivers of glass.

Maybe mine was, too. For seconds hand-running we stood there with the sound of the wind crying through them rocks and nobody batting so much as a eyewinker. His hand fell away. "All right," he said, laughing it off, "you make your point." He flipped the rope off her neck. "Now get out there with Brace and saddle four of those broncs. Whatever's left throw pack rigs on, and don't take more than two weeks to do it."

By six o'clock we was ready to start. Brace and me, mounted, had each of us a saddled bronc to tow and twenty-three others, decorated for packs. You might of thought we was fitting out to go to the moon.

"All set," I grumbled with my look quartering over them. You never seen so many walled eyes in your life. One good sneeze and the whole humped, foot-stomping, head-shaking bunch was like to go kiting off in forty directions.

The girl come out first. Then Jake looking like he'd been pushed through a knothole; then Fisher, spurs flashing, red scarf at his waist, both bone-handled guns and that big silver buckle standing right up between the pushed-back skirts of his coat. He got his grin working again but it didn't get up into his eyes any to speak of.

Dimity said, "Hadn't I better throw together some kind of a meal?" Fisher shook his head. "You can eat when we get back . . . if Jake keeps his mind where he better had."

"Which way we headin?" Fred asked, inscrutable.

Fisher grinned. "Don't think I've gone at this blind, old man. I been up on that mountain. Damn good view. You can look straight across the San Simon Valley, see right into New Mexico without a glass. I found the cave where that bunch is supposed to've played poker. Some graves up there. If it's all the same to you I believe we'll mosey west."

Dimity said, startled, "But Silver Spring —"

"That's the thing about Jake, he's cute," Fisher said, "real cute. Handy with a runnin' iron, too. He can work things over till a ordinary pilgrim couldn't tell Plymouth Rock from Sittin' Bull. And work — God damn! The bones he's moved . . ." He let the rest of it go, staring hard at her. Then his eyes grabbed Fred. "I don't know what's between you two — I don't give a damn. Just get this straight: every time you steer us wrong there's goin' to be something broke. That clear?"

Fred jerked his head.

"All right. Git goin'. Git up there with him, Farsom."

Only thing I found to feel good about was I had my gun back between my legs, the horse I'd rode in here from Tombstone on — Lord, but that seemed a long while ago! Fred was on one of them green-broke broncs, gingerly steering him off through the rocks.

At the pens I come up with him. "This ain't no time to be playin' games," I said. "All the loot in hell ain't worth her losin' a arm or a leg for. That son of a bitch means just what he said."

You could head the broncs shuffling along behind. Fred never turned, never opened his mouth. I suppose I was pretty near beside myself. "If he harms one hair of her head," I snarled, "you better get ready to meet your maker — that's a promise!"

Still not bothering to say anything, he led into the twisting pinch of them walls on the trail down canyon where he'd showed me the bones. I seen a mighty good chance I'd be leaving mine here. If by killing Lupita Fisher'd welded us closer you sure couldn't tell it. He had the whole bunch buffaloed. That kid had showed sense getting out when he could.

If he'd got out. For all I could tell maybe Fisher had killed him, cracked him over the head and shoved him into some hole. He'd been out of my sight long enough to have done it.

Only thing I knew for sure was I'd hit him. Blood . . . we'd all seen it. But if he hadn't been hurt bad enough to stay put — and Fisher hadn't had no hand in what happened, maybe, just maybe, he hadn't took off. Might be the gimpy fool had hid out, hoping someway to get the best of us yet.

Which was all right with me. He hadn't no gun, but a rock, moved right, could do about as much damage in a place like this. It was nothing but wishful thinking, I reckoned, but I begun to perk up, peering around with more notice, hugging to my hopes what I could do with a diversion.

This whole country was dry — powder dry. Even the dusty weeds, what few you could find, was stunted and brittle, falling apart like cracked glass no more than you touched them. In the gray pall kicked up by so many hoofs almost anything might happen if a man stood ready to take a little risk.

I was ready, right enough, but my hands was tied long as Dimity was back there with Brace and Fisher. I kept scouring the rocks for some sign of that kid.

The trail, crooked here as the track of a snake, kept wriggling and winding back into the west. We was headed, I figured, to where I'd worked them damned broncs. They seemed to be doing pretty fair for the moment, coming along without much fuss. Like Fred, up ahead, with his jowls on his shirtfront. I wondered if he'd thought what might happen if they bolted.

I had some other crazy notions in the next couple miles — Fred, too, probably. I couldn't tell what he was thinking but I sure had my eyes peeled. If Fisher was right this old coot could be desperate. And then he scared the hell right out of me.

We'd just come round one of them gooseneck bends and there he was, putting his mount at the wall, twenty-five foot of it straight up and down, the bronc raring back and him slapping the hooks in for all he was able. I said, "For Chrissake!" I thought he'd gone off his rocker, booting that bronc at a clump of dwarf cedar that was all you could see between him and that wall. And next thing I knowed, by God, they was gone — I mean plumb out of sight like they never had been!

I reckon my eyes damn near rolled off my cheekbones.

Back of me them loose broncs was coming up in their pack rigs, and back of them Fisher, and what he'd said would be happening first time he figured he was being crossed up. I was sure enough in one hell of a sweat and it didn't help none when Fred, impatient, growled, "What're you waitin' on?"

I looked all over. I didn't get down on my knees and flippers but alls I could see was these cedars growing out of that great chunk of stone. Then his voice come again, "Push 'em into those bushes!"

If it was hard for me to accept the idea, it was harder still to sell the facts to them broncs. They kept wanting past, trying to get to their bedgrounds. With all that churning and pawing the dust got so thick it was like trapped in the middle of a twister. They didn't break past but not a damn one would go into them cedars. Alls I got from my cuffing and swearing was heads and tails going round and around, and the racket we raised you could of heard clean to Chloride.

I was on the third trip around with my assortment of cusswords when Fisher come larruping out of the dust and, assisted by Brace, with reinends and romal began shoving them through. "Drive 'em into that brush!" Fisher shouted. It come over me then what a kettle of fish we'd of had on our hands if Fred had figured to skin past this hid crack. Made me so weak I pretty near puked.

About the time Brace was waving the last

bronc through I got back enough steam to wonder what had become of Dimity. Spinning around in the leather fetched a look from Fisher that would have set corn to popping. "You can forget that kid — he's probably halfway to 'Frisco."

I didn't disentangle him. I figured I might just as well be agreeable. "I thought," I said, pulling the wipe off my mug, "Fred was clean off his rocker when he piled into them bushes. Mind tellin' me how you got onto it?"

You could see he was tickled. Tapping the crown of his hat he said, "Brains." Then he pointed, "That's Davis Mountain up there, first thing I had to make sure of. Cave's there, and the graves. Soon's I got a look at Hunt's map I knew we was in the wrong canyon; things he described simply wasn't there."

"But the spring —"

Fisher grinned. "By Hunt's description there was *two* springs — remember? I've poked around. This puddle Jake calls Silver is the only piece of water you can find in this gulch. Had to be another canyon; they climbed the mountain to look into New Mexico, so it had to be close. Somethin' else he didn't have was that waterfall. Sure, it might have dried up but there should of been signs. There ain't nothing south, so it had to be a canyon running into Round Valley."

"How'd you know Fred would turn it up for you?"

"It had to be close. If he hadn't made his move

inside the next mile I'd of tackled the girl. I was here a couple months ago, fetching these broncs — seen then he was sweet on her." His grin toughened up. "That makes two of you." He waved me into the cedars. "Better catch up with them."

You could see the opening behind them now that some of the brush had got twisted and trampled. I trailed Brace through. First thing I seen was Dimity up there by Fred hanging onto the horses. She must have gone through while I was fighting that dust.

Brace pushed up the stragglers.

This place didn't look much different than the other except it was greener and maybe, right here, perhaps twenty foot wider. Pretty well haired over. Juniper and live oak mostly. I said to Brace out of the side of my mouth, "You reckon that kid really did cut his stick?"

With his dirty bare feet sticking out of them stirrups all scratched up and clotted he didn't look like nothing a man would put much stock in. His watery glance slithered around. His nose twitched, he snuffled and tugged down his hat to get him out of the sun. "That boy," he confided in his pip-squeak whine, "hadn't no more guts than a junebug."

His lip peeled back and he said, resentful, sounding righteous as hell, "All blat an' no bottom. Even before you loosed that blue whistler the little sidewinder was all set t' crawl off an' leave us!"

Reaching out, Fisher poked him with the end of a finger. "Ride up there with Jake and keep your eyes skinned. And send that girl back."

Pink Cort Brace. A elegant title, I thought, watching him, for as mangy a rat as you would ever find. Then I looked at myself, wondering by how much I assayed any higher. We was all in the same boat . . . except maybe Dimity, I figured, eyeing Fisher.

He grinned at me sourly. "Keep right on hoping. Maybe you can hope Brace out of his pepperbox. Get up there now and keep these broncs moving — don't string 'em out or you'll hear from me."

Dimity come past as I kneed the dun away from him. Our glances touched. I got the notion she was wanting to say something but she reined on by without never a word.

I got the broncs closed up, not chousing them none. Glancing back, I seen Fisher had a rifle across his pommel. I don't know what the hell happened to mine, guess he lifted it probably when he got rid of them others.

The walls was widening out. It was getting hot in here with that sun beating down. There wasn't much dust. Things was moister in here, the broncs breaking their way through a tangle of ash and sycamore. I kept scanning the walls for a way up out of it without finding nothing a goat could use even. I begun to wonder about Fred. Didn't look like anyone had ever been in here.

In the next quarter mile we got a lot more

elbow room. You couldn't see the mountain, but through the leaves of the trees and where it was open there seemed to be places where a feller on foot — if he kept his wits about him — might get up that east climb.

About the time I noticed the broncs slacking off, Fred stuck up a hand. We seen him waggle it at us. Fisher said, "Hold 'em," and, scowling, pushed on with the girl. She was one thing he wasn't about to forget.

Even I could see the excited look on Brace's face. Fred's jaw flapped as Fisher come up with them. I like to ruptured a ear trying to catch what he was saying. Fisher, after a minute, stood up in his stirrups and took a long look around. Shaking his head he pulled aside, waving them on.

I could smell the damp before I got up there. "Silver?"

Fisher shrugged. "We'll know pretty quick. Ought to be a burnt wagon — a hub, anyways. Might be nothin' but spokes. Keep your eyes peeled."

He pushed after the others.

He didn't have to tell me. Maybe it hadn't showed like it had on Brace's face but he was plenty keyed up. Three million smackers!

"Jesus Christ!" I said, and looked around for something I could use to turn the tables. Nobody had to tell me a damned thing. Once he come onto that loot he'd have about as much use for the rest of us as a gray squirrel would have for a load of them minnie balls.

XXI

It was Dimity found the next of Hunt's clues.

She had her bronc out a ways from the others; trying, I reckoned, to get enough room to think in, lallygaggin' along like a sorefooted turtle.

The tinhorn and Fred had pulled ahead a good piece and it was my notions she might be figuring I'd catch up. Seemed like Fisher might be hugging the same idea. He was staring straight at her when she hauled to a stop. Right away he was reining Fred's grulla over, with the old man and Brace twisting round in their saddles.

"Gum Spring," she called.

She must of had good eyes. It was nothing but a green-scummed seep maybe two foot across and just about buried in a clutter of granite chunks off the rim.

"Boys," Fisher grinned, "we're gettin' close."

Their excitement was contagious. Even Fred, I seen, was beginning to breathe hard. It was like I was perched on some high bare place hanging on by two toenails in a buffeting gale. The glare was sky and sun, probably two-thirds fright. The reds and grays and maggoty yellows, with the pale greens shimmering below and above, was the whopper thorns I had fell among that could without half trying rip a man to the bone. It was like I was wide awake in a dream, bare naked and everyone around me dressed. Even the smells was louder, like the hot iron stink coming off that fried ground. It was like I had seen the end of the world and no one but fools could talk my lingo.

Time had about run out. They was going to come up with this goddam plunder. All at once I knew — I could feel the grate of it between my teeth . . . and something else, coldly wicked, like bright little wires boring into my back.

It done me no good to look. There was nothing to see but the rocks and brush and that white crack of sky. Just the wriggle of heat writhing up through the catclaw. Nothing at all I hadn't peered at before.

Fisher waggled a arm. "Forget them broncs. Get up here and help us hunt for that wagon."

I toed the dun over, being careful not to let my glance stray towards Fred. It didn't make no difference. "Old man," Fisher said, "you been in here. Where is it?"

Fred looked like he'd reached the end of his rope.

"Well?" Fisher snarled. Each strike of his stare was like a coiled rattler, wound up and ready.

Fred went back a step, cringing. He'd got off the damned bronc. His eyes crept to me. The knuckles of his hands where they was wrapped through the reins couldn't of been squeezed no tighter.

Fisher's hard stare tramped over my face. I expect all of them was watching — sure felt like they was. A wild fury clawed through me and I come off the leather, straight up in my stirrups . . . and seen the black snout of that unwinking rifle.

I dropped back, all the rage and the shame of it bottled inside me.

What Fred said I never heard. If Fisher laughed I never noticed. Hoof falls and the screak of saddles presently cut through what had hold of me. I seen we was on our way again, still pointing north, riding through gravel as the canyon bent east and the look of things changed, the walls pinching in, the floor strewed with granite, brushy with reefs of manzanita and catclaw that ripped at our pantslegs and tore free, slaty green. There was yucca, too, and pincushion pear, and jumbles of cholla reaching to prod the unwary. Then the view loosened up and Fisher grinned. "There's your waterfall."

I didn't see no water. Just a nest of black rocks heaved up out of the ground in a tangle of broken sticks and dead weeds, and Brace's jaw hanging open. Like the rest I followed Fisher's look to the rim. "It ain't runnin' now," he said in that told-you-so voice. "But there's where she come from and here's where she hit."

We was in a dry wash — I seen that much. And,

against the east wall, the mark of high water. I see Fred staring like a hard-hooked fish. If ever a man looked sick it was him.

Fisher herded us on. I glanced back a couple of times and seen Fisher's teeth. Wasn't nothing else to see but them loose broncs clattering after us. Though I quartered both rims, every patch of brush, each crack and cranny without spotting a thing, the notion kept gnawing. If the goddamn fool didn't hurry it up . . .

It was Fisher and his guns that finally opened my eyes. All the way from Fred's place I'd been determined Alamagordo would someway get the best of him and save us. But why should he? What did he care about Dimity, or even Brace? No skin off his butt if Fisher gunned the lot of us. The kid was after that plunder and alls he had to do was keep out of sight, wait till we found it, then step in and pick up the pieces.

These was the plain hard facts.

You might shut your eyes, talk all around, but when the last chip was down they was what you had to reckon with. Fisher wasn't going to split that loot up with nobody. No help from Brace. Fred . . . well, the fact that he'd showed us the way through them bushes pretty well spoke for him. Any help to be looked for was going to have to come from me, and there wasn't any question but what Fisher figured likewise. Not once had I caught his eyes off me.

It was Brace discovered all there was of the wagon. Two spokes, a iron rim and what was left of a hub. He got them out of the wash. It wasn't surprising we didn't find more. The hub had been half eaten by fire.

The girl looked at Fred like she couldn't believe it. I suppose I had known all along Fred was Gauze. If I hadn't I certain sure should of when he'd parted them bushes.

I had thought when Fisher gunned Lupita it would bring the rest of us closer together. Nothing I could see give any evidence of this. I couldn't afford any more wrong guesses. Gauze, despite the girl's unwavering loyalty, had to be looked at for what he was, a coyote, bold and cunning enough among dogs and women but a mighty sorry sight now that a wolf had sat down on his doorstep.

Brace had a pistol, if I could get my hands on it. He still had that pepperbox he'd poked in my face the first time I'd seen him.

Why had Fisher let him keep it? A whim? Or out of the vast contempt a man of his caliber would feel for a tinhorn? Fisher wasn't a fool; there'd be more to it than that. It probably give him a laugh.

I could see how it would. Curly Bill in his time — he'd been another who'd took a heap of fun out of fools, had frequently pulled some pretty wild stunts for laughs. More likely, I thought, Fisher'd left Brace his pepperbox to make him feel useful, to make him think he was counted on, a part of the boss man's plan. A Judas steer. A kind of pardner.

Why not? That way he could get some use out of the feller. He already had; he'd got his broncs rounded up, the horses he'd had Fred pasture to have them handy when the time come for riding off with Curly Bill's loot.

"Now, Jake," Fisher said, "you get out Hunt's map an' take another look at the positions of these things we've got pinned down. Get them firmly in mind. The next job we're givin' you is to dig up the rock with the two crosses on it. We're countin' on you taking us pretty much right to it."

He showed his teeth. Gauze stood there a minute, then he climbed on his horse with the sweat popping out of him and, never bothering with the map, let off up the wash. He had the look of a man on his way to Armageddon.

Fisher waved me after him, then the girl, leaving Brace and himself to bring up the rear. Near as I could figure, from what I'd seen, we might have as much as a mile to go. We was headed straight in toward the mountain now, coming up from the west. Dead ahead of us it was, the bare rocks sticking out of it like busted ribs.

Maybe, I thought, he'd let Brace keep it in the hope it might push me into showing my hand. Wasn't a chance with him watching I could get the thing away from Brace. Any try I made would give Fisher the excuse to put me out of this deal for keeps. I didn't see, however, that I had much choice.

Ain't a prospect many dwells on, not being around any more for java. Dying is for others, never for yourself. What was it like to cash in your chips? Was there something really waiting for a man beyond the quick?

I hadn't thought much about it, didn't figure to find any time for it now. Something had to give, and soon, or we was done for.

Fisher still had Dimity up at the front but she'd been dragging her feet again. Brace wasn't two horse lengths behind, Fred abreast and me maybe fifty foot nearer the hard shape of the rifle.

There was a dispirited droop to the look of her shoulders that told better than words the kind of thoughts she was stuck with. She set that bronc like a sack of oats, all the jounce gone out of her. My eyeballs quivered, I could feel the breath piling up in my throat. She was nearer already to Brace than she had been.

It come over me like a bundle of sticks, she was shaping a play to get hold of that pepperbox. Near scared the goddam liver right out of me.

It just might work if I could keep that big . . .

I pulled off to the side, rolling a smoke while I set there. Up he come, curious as a cat and twice as leery. "What do you reckon you're up to?" he says, swiveling that rifle to where with one squeeze he could puncture my tintype. "I give you your orders."

"Only one thing," I said, sidling my horse

around to where his eyes couldn't take in the both of us. I seen his suspicion, the wicked jump of his muscles.

Brace's yell climbed like the squeal of a shoat. Fisher'd come too near to back off in time now. My foot hit the rifle just before it went off, tearing it out of his grip. Then I was onto him, slugging and falling as the weight of my dive took him out of the saddle.

It was hard where we fell. I caught the worst of it. Pain roared through me like the rip of barbed wire. He squirmed loose, rolling clear. I tried to come off my back but it was like that rock had busted my shoulder. That damned right arm wouldn't mind me at all.

Frantic, I come onto one knee. A heap of things come into my mind — I even seen my old man. Then the world exploded in a burst of white sparks.

XXII

Much as anything, I reckon, it was the jolting finally roused me; the lurch and roll, the sagging twist, the nerve nagging churn of continual motion. Takes a while, sometimes, to catch up with yourself. The swush of hoofs beat through my head. Hairy legs, a lathered shoulder and heaving ground took up most of the view. I was folded face down across the hug of a saddle.

I wasn't right sure I wouldn't just as lief be dead. I'd never had such aches. I seen the hands flopping around. I must of looked at them half a mile before I noticed they was mine. I wiggled the fingers, first the left then the right. I was kind of surprised to find that both sets worked. Then I remembered Fisher. When I couldn't stand no more of it I got myself up into the saddle.

He must of beat the bejasus out of me. I hung on with both hands, and when the dizziness passed there he was, right alongside of me. He said, "I figured, by Gawd, you was smarter than that."

She was up ahead with a stick thrust between

her back and her arms. They had her hands tied again. Fred was bound, too. I could hear the grunts of the climbing horses. The side of that mountain wasn't a quarter mile off.

The collapse of our attempt at turning the tables had restored all his confidence. You'd have thought by his tone he had that loot in his pockets.

Brace, when Dimity had jumped him back yonder, had snatched out his pepperbox and then, what with the horses acting up and trying to fight off the girl, had dropped the damn thing. It was lost now, gone down a crevice. Only guns in the crowd was the ones in Fisher's holsters and the rifle he'd picked up and had back across his lap.

He said, "I'm tellin' you this so you'll know where you stand." He made it real plain. "You want dirt throwed into their faces just try something else. It ain't going to take more than two of you to load it."

I guess he had a right to feel good.

The east wall petered out against the side of the mountain. It was climbable here, the glare broken up by the shadows of ash and sycamore. Above was fire and piñon and, in between, the blue-black-green of juniper. It stacked high for looks with the light filtered through that leafy tangle of branches.

It was here Fisher found the rock with two crosses.

We spent half a hour lolling around while he

sized up the place, studying Hunt's map and estimating distances. A dozen times he jumped up to poke around, not saying a thing, just looking.

I thought if he would only put down that rifle . . . but he never did. He never come near enough. Unless Alamagordo took a hand in this go-around we had come to the end of our rope it sure looked like.

Fisher, stepping back with his eyes cold and mocking, said, "That kid ain't going to copper no bets. I busted him over the head back yonder."

Something seemed to let go inside Fred. I seen all the lines of his face run together, and the clothes hanging to him looked more looselike than ever; and I wondered if he had made with the kid the kind of a deal he had shoved at me.

"Brace, get the pick," Fisher said, thinly smiling, "and a couple of shovels off that apron-faced roan."

Dimity sniffed. "You're wastin' your time."

Beneath them bold eyes Fisher's grin was like velvet. "You fix your mind on stayin' healthy, anything harder than that I'll take care of." His look bit at me. "Grab up that pick and get over there where you can touch those two crosses."

I felt like a man walking over cracked ice. When I come to the rock he said, "You see that old slide?"

"You mean against the west wall?"

"Sometimes I wonder how I ever done without you. Now, accordin' to this map, Bill's plunder ought to be about midway between where you're at and that slide."

I couldn't sight too good with all them trees sticking up. "You want I should find how many steps it is?"

"Just start hikin'. I'll tell you what I want."

I went around the first boles making sure he was able to see me. The next was a sycamore, two foot through. I could feel the sweat rolling down my back. "While you're wonderin'," Fisher purred, "just recollect what can happen to that girl if I squeeze this trigger."

The son of a bitch thought of everything.

"Right there ought to be about right," he said presently. "Lumpy, ain't it?"

"You think all this chaparral's got growed over it?" I growled, disgusted. "Some of this stuff's two inches across."

"Some of it's dead, too. Start swingin' that pick."

Just bucking that brush was a chore in itself. The ground was like flint and lousy with stones, some bigger than melons. A lot of that growth was green and springy and the goddam thorns didn't make it no easier. When I stopped to mop sweat I'd broke up a patch about ten foot square.

Fisher waved in Fred and Brace with the shovels.

He still had the rifle in the crook of his arm. I peeled off my shirt. "All right with you if I go fetch a drink?"

Eyeing me hard, he said to Dimity, "Get him

the canteen off Jake's grulla."

"Tied up like this?"

"It ain't me that's wantin' it."

She finally got up. Her feet wasn't tied. But her hands still was. "Try usin' your teeth," Fisher said with a chuckle.

I hoped she wasn't going to try nothing crazy. You couldn't tell what that bastard would do. He might shoot to cripple. He might kill her flat out. He had a mighty short fuse and it was already smoking.

I thought back to Lupita. Guts she'd had and a terrible patience, and all she had done knocked hell west and crooked in one squeeze of the trigger when she come up against him.

Who could forget the bright red of her courage or the twist of her look in the flare of that pistol?

The pound of it shook me. I almost cried out when she come to Fred's horse, so wild was my fears, so fierce my imaginings. The moment she stood there seemed to go on forever while my guts shrunk and trembled. My mind yelled *Don't do it!*

When she caught the canteen's strap in her teeth I didn't know whether to shout or swear. I was frantic, I tell you, for a look at his face, but all Tunstall's horses couldn't of turned me then. Her eyes was clear and hard and bright when she passed him with her head held high and come to me through the glare and the shadows.

"That's far enough!" Fisher sharply called while still there was most six strides between us. "Let it go and step back. He can pick it up off the ground if he wants it."

It scairt me the way she fought his will. Then her shoulders sagged, the canteen fell, and she stumbled away with a kind of sob.

Fisher grinned. "Get your drink."

I got off the cap and filled my throat. Then I tossed it to Brace and took up the pick. They had the hole pretty well shoveled out. There was nothing, it seemed, I could do but get at it.

When they cleaned out again we was down two foot. Fisher come and peered in. I tried to think how I might get an edge on him. I seen the glint of Brace's eyes, the scowl on Fred's cheeks. I poked a look up at Fisher. "You think it's deeper'n that? Try it with your foot."

"Cut away that east back a little more," Fisher said.

It was hot stubborn work. Wasn't a breath of wind stirring. The sweat dripped off my nose and chin, off the lobes of my ears and the points of my elbows. You couldn't get him into that pit on a bet.

When I knocked off to ease my aching hips I got that feeling again of being watched.

I rubbed at my kidneys and straightened up slow, taking a long look around. Only eyes meeting mine I could find was Fisher's. Bright as a hawk's and flatter than fish scales.

A bark of a laugh come out of him.

I scrambled up from the hole. The slant of his rifle stayed right on my brisket. "Look," I said, glowering, "we're down better'n two foot. Why don't we try the other side of that rock?"

"Because the mark's over here."

We glared while the quiet got thick enough to chew. "I've about had my fill of your mulishness, Farsom." The bore of his gun shifted blackly to Dimity. "Git back to your diggin."

What the hell could I do? He seen her importance. He savvied how it was, knew the threat was all he needed. I went back to the pick. The worst of it was I had this damnable hunch that before he was done he would knock off the lot of us.

Someone else in his place would of maybe been satisfied — once he'd grabbed onto what he had come for — to set us afoot. But not this whippoorwill. There'd been no call for him to kill that kid. Grounds' death I had laid to Fred's wife because a knife seemed her style, and because she'd been out. But he'd been out too — been practically standing right over him!

Killing was his trade. And, as he'd proved with the kid, he wasn't the kind to leave someone camped on his backtrail.

I banged the pick into that guff like it was him I had under me. I could still feel them eyes, though nothing I come up with offered any real hope this deal was like to get better. A chance could be made, but if it didn't take care of him Dimity would catch the same dose he'd give Lupita. No matter what I figured he was half a step ahead, and no damn way I could see to get up with him.

The fury, frustration — the wild bitterness in me, was sinking that pick to the haft every stroke, breaking the ground up in chunks when I freed it. *Whunk* it would go; then — the whole sound was different — it drove into something that turned it and held it, mighty near wrenching it out of my grasp. Brace had the canteen tilted with his head back, froze with the water bobblin' over his shirt. Fisher, shoving past him, peered down at me, excited.

"Sounded," Fisher said, "like you went through some kind of —"

He must of seen his shadow stretched across the floor of the pit. A second shadow, violently whirling, sent a outflung arm lamming straight for his head. You wouldn't of give Fisher, with that rifle in his dewclaws, any part of a chance. Yet he come around, letting go of the rifle, dropping into a squat, the swish of that arm crazily sailing above him; and there was Cort Brace with his round, frightened eyes of a rabbit off balance, the water still sloshin' in the canteen dangling from its strap at the end of his arm.

A pistol blurred into Fisher's upsweeping fist, fire leaping out of it. Mouth stretched wide in a scream that never come, Brace went half a step back, both hands clapped to his belly. For the moment that he hung there his eyes looked big as slop buckets. Then his knees let go, he come flopping towards me, pushing a path through the dirt with his face.

I guess I jumped back, Fisher's pistol swiveling after me like a snake winding up for a second strike. Dimity screamed. The pistol flew from his hand. From behind and above us the crack of a rifle bounced off the west wall in a clatter of echoes.

We all stood there speechless. The wisp of a mocking laugh drifted down, ugly as gar soup thickened with tadpoles. "Want to try for the other one?"

Fred looked like he wasn't two steps from crazy. All the fires of hell was blazing in Fisher but he was foxed this time, caught flat footed with his back to a rifle and a shooter that had proved he needn't take no sass off anyone. Fisher had one chance, one hand fit to grab it, and no idea where the feller had spoke from.

Wild is one thing. Being loco is for fools and Fisher never was that. He could toss in his hand or get salivated. Way he got shucked of that belt was plumb careful.

Well, Fred had told us. Now we seen the living proof. Just the same I was some surprised when this burly six-footer limped into the open — not so much at his dark beefy face as at the whacked-off pantsleg and the bloody rag twisted around that hairy thigh. Surprised because it was plain enough now I never had dropped that rattlebrained kid; it was Curly Bill Brocius I had put my slug into.

Never mind — this was *him*. You had only to look at Fred or the froze disbelief anchoring Fisher in his tracks. If this wasn't enough consider his shape, the round swarthy face so often described, them black eyes and dimples and ragged shock of raven hair. The sureness of him, the bold clap of his stare. There never was another like Curly Bill.

Thinking about that hole I'd put in him I wasn't a heap more comfortable than Fred. By repute he was chancy as a shedding snake, and just about as chummy when paying back a grievance. But right then all his notions must of been hard-tied to that treasure. His look was crammed with an immense satisfaction as he put us to clearing that plunder of dirt.

Like most tales of booty it had grown somewhat in the telling but there was more than you'd expect. Then two images, almost lifesize. A cigar box filled with precious stones — not all diamonds by a jugful. Round a hundred thousand in negotiable coin, a half-dozen chunks of melted-down silver and forty-one bars of gold bullion. Enough to have kept most of us in chicken for a while.

Time we got it all loaded we was pretty well pooped, all but Curly who'd done nothing more taxing than push out his talk from behind the black bore of that screecher he carried.

While we'd been packing the stuff he had got himself onto Fred's chesty grulla. Fixing Fisher with his stare he motioned the rest of us back. "Mount up, sport. You're trailin' with me till we git some of the ginger worked out of this caballado."

He showed the rest of us his dimples in a parting grin. "A heap worse could happen if we meet up again."

The employees of G.K. Hall hope you have enjoyed this Large Print book. All our Large Print titles are designed for easy reading, and all our books are made to last. Other G.K. Hall books are available at your library, through selected bookstores, or directly from us.

For information about titles, please call:

(800) 223-1244
(800) 223-6121
To share your comments, please write:

Publisher
G.K. Hall & Co.
P.O. Box 159
Thorndike, ME 04986